I0679706

Francis Bay

a novel by

Marshall Evans

Copyright © 2020 by Marshall Evans

All rights reserved. This book or any portion thereof
may not be reproduced or used in any manner whatsoever
without the express written permission of the publisher
except for the use of brief quotations in a book review.

Printed in the United States of America
First Printing, 2020

ISBN 978-0-9970127-4-3

Land's Ford Publishing
Spartanburg, SC, USA

Cover photo by Marshall Evans
Author photo courtesy of Sam Hillers

This is a work of fiction. Names, characters, places, and incidents
either are the product of the author's imagination or are used
fictitiously. Any resemblance to actual persons, living or dead,
events, or locales is entirely coincidental. Public figures in this story and
locations in the Caribbean are used fictitiously

To Hobbs

Had I the heavens' embroidered cloths,
Enwrought with golden and silver light...

   - Aedh Wishes for the Cloths of Heaven

When we've been there ten thousand years,
Bright shining as the sun,
We've no less days to sing God's praise
Than when we'd first begun.

   - Amazing Grace

1

Have you ever had to dispose of a human corpse? If you're an adult, you probably have. Lucrative industries are built around the disposal of dead bodies, providing their living customers ultimate convenience and emotional ease. The messy stuff (and boy, is it messy) is left to pros. As the person who needs to be rid of a corpse, you just have to work on adjusting your memories of the deceased. You'll want to gloss over much of the awful reality as you navigate your public mourning rituals.

You'll have plenty of time to wrestle with the truth later.

But there are corpses you can't send to the funeral home. I'm talking about the corpse who was alive just a few moments ago, before you smothered the life out while the victim kicked and scratched your arms.

Say you had no choice but to get rid of this person. Say the person was the most beautiful, vivacious young woman- and your continued livelihood, maybe your continued existence as a human yourself, depended on the...

Murder.

Oh, sure, you can distance yourself from me now. You've probably never had to murder anyone to hold on to your career.

But it's probable- highly probable- you've gotten rid of someone, one way or the other, because your job and your finances depended on it.

Surely you can summon up that remembrance of things past. This doesn't necessarily make you a horrible person. It makes you a person. It's part of the reality, of the ultimate truth, of having a career of almost any kind.

You know how it's done. You pretend to be trustworthy. You pretend to be a friend. But your mission has already been made clear to you. The other has to go. You have to do it deftly, and you have to clean up the aftermath neatly, or those who forced you do the dirty work may use the evidence of your misdeed as a convenient excuse to get rid of you, too.

Unpleasant thoughts, here, but it's reasonable to assume you have some firsthand experience with this truth.

Well, since I've got you thinking a bit like I do, just let your imagination range a bit further, and you should be able to imagine having an actual corpse to dispose of.

If, say, it's a young woman, and if, say, she had a propensity for fashionable dressing, so she arrived at the place of her death with a couple of large, roll-aboard suitcases, then a solution begins to present itself.

You need a sharp knife. A good quality chef's knife will do. And a hacksaw. Easy finds- they're just one, quick shopping trip away. Some heavy-duty garbage bags.

And a bathtub.

I sincerely hope you'll have to use your imagination here. I hope you don't have any firsthand knowledge of this operation. I'll briefly describe the process to you, but the truth is far more vile, far more shocking, I assure you. The body is still quite warm. The fluids that ooze out and smear the tub and your hands and your forearms are warmer than the corpse's skin. The tendons and ligaments can be tough cutting. You're trying to control the mess, to get the pieces into the garbage bags, to get the bags tied tight, to get everything stuffed into the suitcases without any traces that might alert anyone you encounter during transport.

You've got to leave space for the concrete mix in each suit-case. The sea is a marvelous, fine place for hiding things in ev-erlasting mystery. You will buy the concrete mix on another quick shopping expedition, after you have the suitcases in the car. That makes the luggage lighter to transport in public. Say you had a hundred-and-twenty-pound victim. You've let about fifteen pounds run down the bathtub drain. That leaves two very hefty suitcases to wheel to the car and heave into the trunk- in plain view of any passersby.

You'll want to add the concrete mix later. In a private place.

And the sea will provide the water.

Grisly, you may be thinking.

Inhuman, you may think.

Psychopath! you may think.

Intelligence operative doing his job, I think.

I know the truth behind this kind of work. And I'm just getting up the nerve to write about it.

2

Francis Bay may be the most beautiful place on Earth. I've traveled all over. I'm an old man.

I came to this conclusion when I was there with two friends on my boat. The friends will remain anonymous, but that day, under the influence of sufficient rum, we reached agreement that Francis Bay just might be the most beautiful place we had ever seen. One friend had sailed in the Marquesas. The other had sailed to Bora Bora and Moorea. I had helicoptered into the remotest corners of the Peruvian Amazon and Patagonia... God, I've been more places than you can imagine. This was the most beautiful.

A ruin sits high on a hill above Francis Bay. The crumbling mansion is said to have been a residence of the brutal Dominican dictator Trujillo. If an evil, ruthless man of unlimited, pilfered wealth chose this as his vacation spot, well...

Speaking of ruthless people with pilfered wealth, there is an entire development of homes- not yet ruins- overlooking Francis Bay slightly more to the West. These sprawling palaces cling to the mountainsides right in the middle of the Virgin Islands National Park, protruding in twenty-first century garishness from the protected forest. It's one of the most expensive and exclusive neighborhoods in United States territory.

On a small island at the entrance to the Bay, there is a lone ruin, a former customs house. There is a good bit of voodoo paraphernalia there, and the place is haunted by myriad, powerful jumbies.

On September 6, 2017, the eye of hurricane Irma, then the fiercest storm ever recorded in the Atlantic, passed a couple of miles north of Francis Bay. The best part of this story happened less than a year after that storm passed. The tropical rain forest on the mountainsides had been shredded by Irma. We could still see the devastation nearly a year later. Trunks were bare. Trees were leveled. Debris was piled high. Now, nine months after the storm, the forest was just beginning to turn green again. It rang with noises, sounds, and sweet airs.

Coqui frogs were so loud in the night you'd think jumbies were flying and dancing in the wildest of reveries, shrilling and whirring in the trade winds. At least I'd think that.

The sea turtles had returned to Francis Bay after the storm. Lots of sea turtles.

The National Park Service maintains moorings for private yachts in Francis Bay. After Irma, the Park Service declared the moorings open for an entire season. Rangers temporarily stopped enforcing the rule that boaters could spend no more than two weeks at a time in any one bay in the Park. Mooring fees were waived.

So I found myself for several months that year moored in the most beautiful place on earth, passing my days and nights in a vortex of cavorting jumbies above, and silent, serene sea turtles grazing and gliding beneath me.

And knowing, honestly, that I was a dead man.

3

I knew my hospitalization would be the end of things with the agency. The intern asked if I might still consider harming myself, and in one crazy moment of honesty, so completely out of character for me, I told him, "Yes." As a result, they put me in the lock-down ward. Heavy sedation turned me momentarily into some kind of pathetic, trusting child. It dulled my senses and my scheming just enough to make me surrender.

I wanted so badly to be honest. I wanted so badly to trust someone.

Joyce had brought me to the hospital. I wanted so to trust her. Joyce doesn't lie. She doesn't scheme. She doesn't understand most of what I tell her even now about the agency. And Joyce understands even less of what I tell her about the supernatural. She's a wrinkled, beautiful ingenue.

Joyce. There's a complicated subject.

I was fed enough Paxil to send me into a suicidal spiral, Joyce answered my call and drove me to the hospital. She hugged me and pressed her lips against my bald head. I cried on her shoulder. I sobbed. She took me to the emergency room, where I had the aforementioned spasmodic episode of loose lips with the young intern, and soon I heard the click of an electronic lock closing behind me, the nurse detachedly demanding I remove my belt and shoe laces. I sobbed again as I handed them to her.

That is what precipitated the end of my intelligence career. It's what began my being cured. It began my journey into a world of truth. Which was fundamentally different from the endless whirlwind of fiction I had inhabited up until that point.

4

I'm skipping at random through the story here. Time is irrelevant. The story is what counts.

Here is a poem I wrote some twenty-eight years ago.

On the Healing Power of Prayer Directed to the Almighty
On Our Behalf By the Holy Mother of God

by
Francis Bay

The subject of this afternoon's lecture
Is: Just
How much can the impenetrably esoteric
Fog I am about to blow
Into this room
Condense upon the vanity
Of your intellectuality
Like droplets of sea-mist
On Namibian desert plants,
Sustaining life where it shouldn't be?

Oh, blast it all. I want to tell you,

But would that be the end of everything?

I was flying home
from Warsaw once (on a final leg
from Chicago,) when I found myself
alone on the plane with a group of pilgrims
who had missed their connecting
flight returning from Medugorje.
And in the darkness
a priest told me:
at Medugorje
he had become convinced
that the world we live in
is only half-sight,
that the true world is the spiritual world,
and that I should go to Medugorje
to witness the apparitions of the Virgin
if I possibly could,
so that I might see these things for myself.

I've never been.

But now, here is the truth,
and this is very hard to tell.

Some nights, when I am in the bed
beside my wife and I close
my eyes and say silent prayers,
the Mother of God comes in her golden robes,
gliding at first on the clouds,
coming over the edge of the world,
and then coming closer, into our bedroom,
so that I cannot open my eyes from fear.

She is in our room, holding her arms out
over our bed,
and she says in her smile
that all will be well,
and God loves me.
So now, that is what the truth looks like.
Would you rather hear my lecture?

There's some fiction in this poem. Except for the last part, which is all true. And except for my eponymous name, which is true and not true.

It's probably easiest if you just call me Francis Bay. Many people have.

She came again last night. This time there were no golden robes. She was a simple Jewish girl who had been impregnated by God, who had watched her son be tortured and murdered, and who had lived to be old.

She told me to tell this story. I had no choice, really.

5

It's hard for me to tell where the lies end and truth begins, really. My mother used to tell me, on those rare occasions when I'd stop in to see her in that God-awful house in North Charleston, "Welcome back to the real world." She said that every time I walked in her door as an adult. As if that shithole with its grimy walls and weedy yard was in any way the real world.

Almost immediately on my escape from college, I had begun living in what I always imagined was the real world. Dahran. Hong Kong. Dubai. Palawan, for God's sake. Even boring little Santiago, where my apartment offered stunning views of Manquehue and Cerro El Plomo. It was all vastly more spectacular than anything my mother ever knew. No wonder all the men she married left her. No wonder.

Actually, that was precisely the problem. No fucking wonder.

I, on the other hand, found wonder. Working as a deep-cover operative, living in the safe homes they bought me, frolicking in the permanent immunity from IRS probing and auditing. I wondered at the astonishing ease with which I could borrow money or move it around internationally- or simply invent it when I felt it necessary.

I wasn't a good businessman. But I was an excellent scammer. I've always been that.

(I wonder if that's entirely the truth.)

This experience with the truth is so new in my life that I don't have much perspective on it.

Back to Francis Bay.

Why were all those jumbies swirling and cavorting around me?

Jumbies, if you don't know, are forest spirits in Caribbean animist religions. The concept came originally from Africa. Maybe the jumbies themselves came from Africa. Those characters walking on stilts in Caribbean Carnival parades are called "mocko" jumbies. They're impersonating the real thing.

I lived my life as a mocko man. I impersonated a real man. And now, in Francis Bay, I probably had a couple of months to try to actually *be* real. I had no idea how one might do this.

When I talk about jumbies, the real ones, that were inhabiting the most beautiful place in the world in those final weeks, I am not inventing something. I'm trying to talk to you truthfully. Believe me, this is not an easy thing for a sixty-year-old man to begin doing out of the blue. But I am trying.

6

Jumbies are the souls of dead people stolen by obeah-men. Jumbies have to roam the night forests looking for evil to do to living people.

Jumbies jump into cats and bats and such creatures and attack people. I watched a cat attack a middle-aged tourist on St. John, once. The tourist was walking in Cruz Bay wearing shorts and Birkenstocks.

The cat jumped onto the man's naked leg and clung with all four sets of claws. The man kicked and screamed and cursed. The cat howled and clung.

In its own time, the jumbie let go and ambled across the street. It ducked between two buildings and disappeared.

A street full of tourists gathered round the wounded man in outrage, worried the animal posed a public health risk. The man and his wife held each other in fury. He was bleeding from claw marks. He was worried about infection. He feared rabies.

He should have been worried a jumbie had sucked the spirit out of him.

The West Indians who witnessed this may well have been worried about it. They stood a moment in stunned silence. Then they scattered in all directions.

I just laughed.

Strange tale, you may think, coming from an intelligence agent. You imagined, perhaps, we would be more... Rational? Stable? Sane? Really?

Have you ever known an intelligence agent?

Have you ever lived knowing a Russian assassin could come at any moment to end your life?

How often do you worry about Novichok nerve agent swiped on your door knob?

On your dinghy motor in a place like Francis Bay?

I have known "intelligence operatives" of all stripes and nationalities the better part of four decades. "Sane" and "rational" are not two words that jump to mind.

I can think of a number of words that are more apt. "Abused." "Psychopathic." "Pathological." "Twisted." "Fragile." "Paranoid." "Neurotic." "Psychotic." "Squirrelly."

Or better yet: "emanating a sort of psychic smell, a rancid intellectual odor that the recruiter of spies can detect wafting on zephyrs as his prey approaches."

We detect them as easily as a sexual predator can spot a mark.

We- the dedicated professionals engaged in this sort of work- simply know who we are. And we can spot those who are destined to play our game. We barely even have to think about it.

I can't believe I'm writing these things down. These are the kinds of things a man like me simply can't write about. This kind of honesty is stupid and dangerous.

But I'm not afraid of being killed, now. I'm not afraid of financial ruin or public ridicule or career destruction.

Like Jose Marti's *hombre sincero*, before I die, I want to toss out the verses of my soul.

I am a sincere man, now.

7

Or am I a man without nothing? I've always liked that play on words in Marti's most famous poem. *Un hombre sin cero.*

I can speak eight languages fluently. Yes, fluently. Three or so- Spanish, French, and Portuguese- I can speak idiomatically. What was the point of all that? You could say it was in furtherance of my profession- but I'm not sure that's so. See, the reality of working in American government or business is that being able to speak any language other than English makes you suspect.

The majority of people, the people in charge, can't do it of course. They think you are casting magical spells, conspiring with the foreign devils against them. They don't really trust you.

For God's sake don't learn another language, I want to tell young people. If you're Dutch or Norwegian, you can do it, but not if you're American. You'll spend your whole life riding lonely on the frontiers.

Eight languages? You may be thinking. How in the world can he do that? It takes a bit of determination and hard work in the beginning. It surely takes some native aptitude.

You'd wonder, perhaps, if having the ability to render thought and spirit into so many different languages would make communication any easier. Can the polyglot more easily reach out and touch others, bring them into that fleeting intercourse of the soul we achieve when we discover, if only for a flicker of a moment, what the other is feeling?

I haven't noticed that it does.

Knowing many languages may open up understanding of other cultures. But understanding other cultures puts you at a distinct disadvantage if you're an American. Because most Americans don't understand other cultures.

I digress. I was talking about Francis Bay. But in reality all I can do is digress. When one is moored in Francis Bay, one enters a kind of limbo, where digression and the serendipitous exploration of the soul are rampant on a field of clear cerulean. A couple of glasses of Zacapa rum on the rocks with a slice of lime. Twenty-four to forty-eight hours in close company with a companion or two on a sailboat, scooting across the bay in a dinghy, walking the brilliant white sand on the beach, swimming and snorkeling in the transparent water, floating silently with grazing sea turtles, holding one's breath for a closer look...

Soon the universe is nothing but a gigantic digression. Time and causality melt into a continuum of what...?

Listen to those tree frogs' screams. The jumbies' howls.

Sure, my friends. Let's have another glass of rum. Look at the Milky Way, beginning to lose its tail to the moonlight looming beyond the mountaintops.

Yes, kick back in the cockpit. Now, friends, tell me those secrets from your childhood. The ones we never even shared when we were boys in college. Your mother kissed you with her open mouth, you say? You say it with disgust. She slipped in her tongue? There are tears in your eyes, now, and tears in mine, and I think of the women we shared. God, I didn't want to remember that, catching you drunkenly in the eye as we moaned at either end of the mystifying co-ed.

We really don't want to go to all these places, do we? Weren't we just talking about surrender to the Almighty? To the good and the all-knowing font of eternal beneficence?

Can rum and ice and lime, and the countless stars whirling slowly over Francis Bay at midnight do these things to us?

Perhaps we should go to how the Russians got their hooks so deeply into me. That will pull us back down to a bit of temporality and causality, and maybe that will help.

8

It seems to me one of the most useful traits a person can have in intelligence is a thoroughly muddled sense of the boundary between good and evil.

I've known people, my wife Joyce being perhaps the best example, who seem to have some sort of innate knowledge of good and evil. Joyce is comfortable sizing up every situation and every person she comes into contact with. If a course of action or a situation will lead to evil, she seems to sense that, and she naturally and confidently veers away. If a person is evil, she handles them at a safe distance.

I really can't clearly distinguish between good and evil. I'm never quite sure which is which. When I look straight into the face of evil, whether I'm looking at a human face or evil configured in a situation, I just can't be certain. I keep seeing this possibility of good in it. Even where there is no possibility. Time and again, throughout my life, I stared straight in the face of the barest, vilest forms of malevolence. Invariably, I perceived some possible good- good that may or may not have been there. Who knows? I displayed a lifelong knack at allying myself with the forces of evil- through my own misguided optimism.

This is not the sort of thing you might expect to hear from an agency man. But I think it may actually be one of those subtle, smell-able traits that make a soul ripe to be recruited into this kind of work. You see, we must be able to convince ourselves our lurid machinations are ultimately for the greater good. At some point we have to believe the politician or the bureaucrat who has committed us to this course of action actually enjoys some sort of moral ascendance. We must tell ourselves (and so many others) we are working for democracy, for the rule of law, for justice, for human rights- for the ideal with which we choose to delude ourselves- when we entice the recruit into the relationship that will eventually destroy his or her life, his or her family, his or her relationship with truth itself.

9

"Francis" Joyce says, "you aren't threatening to write a novel again, are you?"

She laughs. Dismissively.

Wisely, perhaps.

"You're probably going to write a book where you play the Creator, aren't you? People don't want to read that shit, Franny. You need to cut it out. Plus, you know perfectly damn well you can get killed if you even come close to telling the truth."

She's so sensible.

I wrote this poem about her. Or to her. Some thirty years ago, I think. Time again. I'm flitting through time because...

I wrote this poem for her because she couldn't see the things I was telling her about. She longed to see them. The apparitions. The glimpses of heaven. She seemed to believe me when I told her about them, but...

Here's the poem:

To Joyce

by
Francis Bay

Close your ears my love and strain
To hear the melody again.
Airless born the still vibrations
Fill the empty on occasions
When soundless life sounds lifeless.

Hear the muted wood-deer chant?
The batwing's turn? The night-owl's slant?
On the summer breeze you see
The twangling, scented, spring-bloom tree
That sang in white to petals falling,
Spring-dying to the weary calling.

Soft! For there the sweet flesh lies.
May's tender for the greenleaf dies
That shrouds the hot-wood's summer trilling,
Shades the humus, balms the willing.

There the crescent fungus glows.
There the digging beetle knows
(Scratching round the tap root's thrust)
What every grubbing creature must:

That evensong is darkness swelling
Dawn the quick stars' day-rest knelling-
All the silent kingdom's telling
Us to listen, dear.

For we may ear the soundless,
Embrace and squeeze the boundless,
Feeling in our bones the song
For which you, love and heart's hope, long.

    I get pathetically sentimental when I read that now. I suppose just because I'm getting near the end, and it was so long ago. I do love her so.

    There was so much hope and love and pain in that early poem. I just see the hope and love and pain, I think, and I can't really see whether the poetry is good or bad. I'm not sure.

    Now I know how the story unfolded. It's really just overwhelming. The truth. The story. Our lives together. Our marriage.

    I don't know if I can go on with this and make any sense.

10

The love of your life. The idea is probably just fiction. I don't believe we truly have loves of our lives. We fall in love. We may be madly in love for a moment. Then we fall out of love. If we fall out before we're ready, before the love is destroyed by the natural progression of time, then we create nostalgia for the formerly beloved. We imagine into existence- retrospectively- the loves of our lives.

Thus, we sentimental fools perpetuate a fiction: the one perfect, soulmate we were always destined to find.

Hogwash. Joyce and I have had a thirty-year marriage, for God's sake. I know something about the reality of love. It sucks in the long term. It produces children, usually. Those children can go bad. They can die. They can bloody kill themselves, for God's sake. Careers crumble. Finances crumble. Sanity crumbles. Beauty crumbles. What was love becomes a toxic waste site.

Then some gorgeous girl insinuates herself into your life, and after the proper stroking and a few breathless, sweaty couplings, you've concocted the fantasy of having met the love of your life. Your soul mate.

You'd think, after two decades' experience devising schemes to exploit just this kind of self-destructive idiocy in people, I would be love-proof. But I wasn't. I was as desperate and as foolish as anyone.

The approach was the key. It was a brilliant bit of intelligence work. How do you target a hardened professional and slide the agent into his life without his suspecting a thing?

First, of course, you pick your target at the moment when he is most vulnerable.

Perhaps you've had the experience of a teenage child going bad. It happens so quickly. You're at the height of your career. You're traveling the world, doing the work you always wanted to do. People are stroking your ego. You are supremely competent. In your world of work, hardly anyone can touch you.

You have this kid at home. He was a little kid who loved you and admired you. Worshiped you. Hugged you. Kissed you. Wanted to be you.

Then about in the space of an afternoon, he is a lying thug. He spends his waking moments scheming to deceive. He develops secret friends. Secret schemes to get your money. Secret schemes to get clothes you don't want him to have. To get music you don't want him to have. To watch pornography you don't want him to watch. To get drugs. To become the victim of bastards you could see coming miles away if you ever saw them, but by the time you do, they already have your kid firmly in their grip.

I couldn't give it my full attention. I had serious stuff going on in my life. I was saving the United States from a terrorist threat that didn't really exist.

I knew our mission was based on a colossal lie, but the lie fed me the adventure and money and competence and ego stroking I wanted so desperately.

My son had, for several years, fed me something I really wanted. Actual love. Then, almost overnight, he stopped.

When I realized what was going on, it was too late for effective countermeasures. I raged. I worried. I punished. I pontificated. I began to take my frustration out on my wife. She took her own frustrations out on me.

Oh, I don't know if you want to hear the story this way.

Maybe you want to hear it the way we told it in Francis Bay that summer. A few rum drinks. A brilliant, swift sunset. A night sky resplendent with stars and dark clouds. A trade wind. Old men cautiously beginning to let go of the dark secrets they so carefully guard from everyone else. This is how the summer went. This is what made it so different. So special.

11

I met her innocently enough. The daughter of my college buddy.

Ford Cooley was as close to being a real friend as anyone I knew. We didn't see each other that often really- reunions, weddings, a few times we found ourselves traveling overnight in the same city. But we kept in contact, and when we did get together, we chatted like schoolboys long into the evenings. We had each other's email addresses, and later our cell numbers, and we traded jokes and memes. He thought I was in the aerospace business. I knew he was a hydrocarbons broker living outside Houston, with a summer home in Martha's Vineyard.

I was sailing in the Vineyard with Joyce- a desperate attempt to spend some civil time together a year or two after the death of our son. (I can never remember exactly when he died, now.) I wrote to Ford that we would be in town. He invited us to visit. We spent four days with him and his daughter in their vacation home, leaving our boat on a mooring in the harbor.

Ford is divorced. His ex-wife is Bolivian. Fine Bolivian family. Serious money and serious connections. Luisa was an Anthropology grad student at Penn.

Luisa was captivating. Urbane. Immaculately mannered. Former debutante (Ford had a photo in his living room- Luisa in her ball gown at The Pierre.)

And she was so disarming. So ingenuous. Not flirtatious or sexually dangerous. My wife loved her.

It was supposed to be a two-day visit, but it stretched into four days. Under the influence of the Vineyard and a sailboat and a gorgeous house in the dunes, and dinners lingering into the summer evenings, our conversations led eventually into the most forbidden of topics: Ford's divorce, the divorce's effect on Luisa, our son's death.

These subjects were treacherously difficult, but Ford and I shared a college friendship and trust. Luisa had a spectacular talent for getting people to talk about real things. She never had much patience for superficial conversation.

Joyce and I were amazed and receptive.

Luisa was quite talented. The meeting with her seemed so coincidental. I'm sure to this day Ford had no idea I was working for the agency.

I don't want to be irrationally paranoid.

I want to be rationally paranoid. You need to be hypothesizing about these things at all times.

Luisa is dead now. I killed her. Her reputation with her handlers is stellar, no doubt. A loyal agent who gave her life on the job.

12

This is all such a distant distraction from what I really wanted to talk about. I wanted to talk about my summer in Francis Bay. The summer I finally got clear of all this shit. When I entered the Kingdom of Heaven.

Yes, that is terribly presumptuous of me, but what else would you call it? I kept wondering if I was already dead. Seriously. I kept telling people maybe I was already dead, and this summer in Francis Bay with old friends was a spectacular afterlife.

I even ceased to fear the Russian assassin I knew would come some day soon, in some unexpected way. I knew the attempt was inevitable. But it didn't terrify me anymore. It was just another way for me to make the passage we all must make.

The days in Francis Bay passed in timeless and sublime detachment. Old acquaintances came. They went. We swam, we snorkeled, we sailed, we hiked. We dined, we drank, we plunged effortlessly into the type of deep conversation Luisa used to lure my wife and me a few years before in Martha's Vineyard.

I can still remember what led us into that space in the Vineyard. Luisa's father actually started to discuss the raw emotions of his divorce, right there in front of his grown daughter.

Within minutes he was in tears. The failure, the pain, the damage he knew he had done to the people he loved the most. They weren't bad tears. They were uncontrollable tears of joy at having given voice to the pain we carry around and can't allow ourselves to share.

How did Luisa do that?

And how did Joyce join so effortlessly and seamlessly into the conversation, talking about her pain and love with the very man who had caused it all? And in such a way that I did not become defensive?

How does this kind of most profound communion ever spring up?

Is this self-delusion? After all, that conversation at Ford's house in the Vineyard may have seemed like the most sincere and heartfelt of communions, but it was a communion that was prelude to unimaginable betrayal, and, ultimately, to the murder of seemingly the most innocent person in the room.

13

I don't want to be a bad man. I want to be a good man.

I tell myself I have done the right thing. Time and again. But when I step back just a bit and look with the clear vision one sporadically has, I realize I was as filthy and corrupt as can be.

A specific example:

When I was twenty-four years old, working for Fortz, I was given the opportunity to deliver my first foreign bribe. Now, as you may or may not know, bribery paid by U.S. corporations in foreign countries is illegal. Somebody in a U.S. company can go to jail if corporate money is paid as a bribe in a foreign country. So these payments have to be handled carefully.

They are often structured as consulting contracts or payments to local business agents, or as unreasonable mark-ups to local distributors or freight forwarders. But occasionally, in the interest of winning a contract in the heat of the moment, a company such as Fortz, one of the largest defense contractors in the world...

(Defense! Are their products ever really used for defense?)

Anyway, a company like Fortz sometimes just has to put a big, ugly bundle of dollars in a bag and deliver it straight to a foreign crook.

Now, they have to have plausible deniability for this. No vice president or other company officer can be directly involved in the transfer. They need to recruit an expendable fool to do their dirty work for them. They need to sniff out their victim, just as the child molester sniffs out his, and there I was, a twenty-four-year-old engineer on a project in Dahran.

It takes time for the child molester to groom his victim. It took time for Fortz to groom me. They began with praise for jobs well done. Conversations with our feet on the desk at the end of the day. The occasional invitation into the country manager's office on the top floor in Al Khobar.

Then I was included in drinks at an executive's house in the expat compound. The uncorking of the coveted, smuggled bottle of Scotch. The inside gossip about company politics. The dinners where I was the youngest person at the table.

"High-pot," they called me. I had "high potential." They spoke in mysterious ways, as if Fortz had a secret list of "high-pot" young men (surely they would all be young men in those days) tucked away in the Reno headquarters.

A fellow high-pot- a ruthless young Australian prick- once told me there was a locked, windowless room in the basement in Reno, where each of us high-pots had a photo stuck to a wall map depicting the world. There the high priests of Fortz moved us around, ignoring spouses and children and homes and lives, and plotting- what? What the hell exactly? What would any of these supposed high priests stand to gain from such a ridiculous concept?

The lie this young Aussie was telling me was an outrageous, onanistic fantasy. Those old men didn't give a rip about us. They were just jockeying for their own advantage, trying to suck out as much money as they could before they themselves succumbed to the vicious internal politics of the organization, a zero-sum game that allowed only one of them to make it to the top and cling there for a few years, flailing away on all sides at those who would depose him.

Precious few of these old warriors left with enough money to support themselves as they had fantasized for the rest of their lives.

But that's neither here nor there. I may have believed the young Australian's ridiculous fiction, but I was not destined to live the life of a high-pot at Fortz. I would eventually be drawn into the world of a deep-cover agent, with my work at Fortz as nothing more than a cover for my movements around the world. But first, Fortz's country manager for Saudi Arabia had to teach me how to be a whore.

14

He never told me what the payment was for. The country manager's excuse was that if I didn't know what deal Fortz was seeking with the Saudis, I would be far less likely to find myself in deep trouble if I were caught.

I was simply to drive one of the company SUV's into the desert southeast of Dahran, meet a man who would be in a black, S-class Mercedes, engage in a brief conversation containing the passwords "fractal" and "Warsaw," and help the man transfer two rolling suitcases from Fortz's company car to the trunk of his Mercedes.

I was allowed- no, I was pushed- to open the two suitcases to see they were full of hundred-dollar, U.S. bills. Used hundred-dollar bills. I was encouraged to take several stacks out so I could see there was nothing else in the suitcase.

"You've got to be sure what you're doing, Francis," I was told. "You can't do this sort of thing unless you're absolutely sure what you're getting into. What if someone tried to send you to deliver drugs?"

In those years, new arrivals at Dahran airport were greeted by huge red lettering- painted across the exterior walls of the airport terminal where one might expect to see "Welcome to Dahran."

In reality, the bold red letters read, "DEATH TO DRUG TRAFFICKERS."

The country manager didn't have to do a lot of convincing. I did what he said.

This was only a confidence-building gesture. The child molester pretends to care about the handsome, young boy. I was being groomed as a high-pot, alright. A high-potential tool to do their dirty work and then to be cast aside, knowing full well I would never squeal on them.

One vivid memory from my drive out of town: Though I had been in Saudi Arabia several months, this was the first time I had driven in-country. I was on an absolutely empty stretch of freeway- two lanes in each direction- with no cars ahead or behind me. No buildings in sight. Only the one exit ramp I was supposed to take.

In an abundance of caution, I used my right turn signal before I took the exit. Checked the rear view. Nothing. Nobody.

I started to ease toward the exit lane.

A horn blared behind my right shoulder. A black Mercedes sedan passed in the emergency lane, spraying gravel and sand as it slid into the exit ramp. Then it careened back onto the freeway and disappeared into the distance. It must have been going close to two hundred miles an hour.

The near-collision scared hell out of me.

I tremulously took the exit. Found the right road. I drove into the desert until the pavement stopped. I kept driving down a rocky lane far, far out of sight. There a black, S-Class Mercedes was pulled over on the side of the desert track with its trunk open. A solitary man in a thobe and gutra stood beside it, serene in the blazing sunlight.

I got out of the SUV. The man did not appear to be Saudi at all. He spoke English with a thick, Eastern-European accent. I started the most absurd conversation with him. I remember only the two words I was listening for in his response. If I didn't hear those two words, I had been told, I should simply shake his hand, get back in the SUV, and leave.

I heard "Warsaw" early on. I wasn't paying any attention to what the bastard was saying to me. I was only listening for two words. He said "Warsaw," and then he spoke a long time. But I didn't hear the other word.

There was a long, awkward pause.

"It's terribly hot out here," I said, rather dazed.

"The mirages," he said, sweeping his hand toward the shimmering horizon. "Look at them."

The heat danced in the distance like howling jumbies mocking me in the deep desert.

"It's like watching fractals form, isn't it?" he said. His accent was so thick I wasn't quite sure if I had heard the word "fractal." I stared straight into his face.

He smiled serenely at me, without saying another word.

After another long pause in that obscene desert heat, one in which my mouth felt like asphalt on the freeway, I walked to the rear door of the SUV, opened it, and pulled out the two suitcases full of cash.

The man did nothing but smile.

I lugged the two cases to his car. They were heavy- ungainly.

He did nothing to help me. He still smiled the same lurid smile. I didn't want to look at him.

I put the suitcases into the trunk of his car. He closed the trunk, said nothing, and got in the driver's seat. He started the engine and sped away in the opposite direction from which I had come. He drove like a madman, gravel spewing from the rear tires.

I got back into the SUV and turned the vehicle around very, very tentatively on the unpaved track, fearing I would get stuck in the desert sand and die out there. When I was safely headed in the right direction, I drove back to Al Khobar.

I had just survived my first childhood sexual assault. I was a big boy, now.

15

Let's explore a bit more, if you will, this feeling that I was already dead in Francis Bay- that I had quite undeservedly been granted a sojourn in paradise after the end of a miserable life.

I didn't have virgins. I had buddies. Old buddies, ones I hadn't screwed badly enough for them to hate me, who came for days at a time, who swam or sailed or hiked with me during the day. How the hell did I even keep people in my life like that after all I had done?

Mostly I looked them up and revived friendships that had been dormant for decades. Typical. The kind of shit I would do.

These guys didn't know the baggage I carried. And, truth is, once we got to where we could talk, it turned out they all had a good bit of baggage themselves. Real life doesn't run like a fucking novel. It's a goddamn mess.

They talked long into the evenings in the cockpit, then wandered into their bunks as I did, sinking almost immediately into blissful sleep. Stars shone through the hatches above our heads.

The days passed- not without fear. Not without regret. Not without anger or pain, but in a state of surrender and ease that made those omnipresent emotions, my constant companions through a lifetime of deceit and scheming, recede into insignificance. I was aware of them. I was aware they had not gone away. I was under no illusion the basic conditions of the universe had changed.

My companions let go. I let go. Something true was happening to us. Something we were aware of, but I don't think any of us could have explained if we tried.

After all, we were anchored directly in the path of destruction left months earlier by the most intense hurricane ever recorded.

But for some reason, I was- what? I was happy, I think. I had never been happy before. I had never surrendered so completely to God. I was a true Muslim. The thought made me chuckle. Jesus, the world must be full of bastards who would slit my throat and spit on me for saying that. But I didn't care anymore. I didn't really even hate them anymore.

What had happened to me? Several times over those months I told friends of this sensation of already being dead. I laughed. It was the most absurd statement.

They just accepted it with a peaceful smile, and we went on with our friendships.

Nos fecisti ad te, et inquietum est cor nostrum donec requiescat in te...

If Saint Augustine was correct, was I simply resting- where? In God? Saint Ignatius said that all human beings at some point have this sensation, where they abandon themselves into God's hands and feel profoundly at peace, at rest.

Is this what was happening in Francis Bay?

I'd like to try to do it now. Can I get back to that spot?

Sure. I can just let go. Like I'm dropping off the peak of one of the Pitons on St. Lucia. I'm speeding now toward the village of Soufriere far below me. It is the most beautiful human habitation I have ever seen, situated on a breathtaking bay, with the Pitons soaring above.

And it is the most miserable place I have ever seen. The poorest people. The naked kids. The relentless, stoned hustlers and con artists and thieves. The yachts moored offshore. The spectacular, ultra-exclusive resort just around the point. You'd have to pay thousands a night to stay there.

To get through another day in Soufriere, most people have to steal something.

There, I let go. I threw myself from the heights in the most beautiful place I can imagine, and I landed almost immediately in that pain and misery.

Funny. I still feel the sense of peace. Maybe I am dead, now. Maybe I've just moved beyond it all.

How did I get here?

When I was a young man, I fancied myself a poet. Look at these exhibits. I wrote them as an old man in Francis Bay. It had been decades since I wrote a poem.

Coquis

by Francis Bay

Coquis on these summer evenings
Scream forth in pings,
Don't really sing.
But the notes confuse the humid air,
And the human ear
Must resonate in dreams,
For who can hear
The bay trees ring
And feel the is and not the seems?

(Coquis are Puerto Rican tree frogs. They aren't really supposed to live on St. John. But they do.)

Night Sky

by Francis Bay

Starlight brightens nothing
But points of sky
When the night
Horizon zooms to spread the blue-back
Universe around and bright.
The million points of light
Shine and lie
Unaffecting in the chilly void.
But oh the sight!

16

Francis Bay, a poet. That's a stretch.

Why am I giving him those poems I wrote as a very young husband?

I wish I were as eloquent as Nabokov. I wish my evil, unreliable narrator (*my* Humbert Humbert) could make his reader a co-conspirator in his deliciously demented confession...

O.k., so Bay is a fiction. But he really is me. I'm writing this novel about myself, and I'm making the main character fictional. It's liberating. Nabokov discovered when you make yourself into a fictional narrator who is a psychotic sexual predator, you can tell all the fucking truth you want. Nobody can accuse you of being that predator, because if you were... Well, nobody really wants to go there, do they? I mean you'd belong in prison. You ought to be dead. You ought to be assassinated by Russian operatives. You ought to... Well, it's hard to think up just how terrible an end would be fitting for you.

Oh well, it never pays to think fiction through as you're inventing it.

So... here I was, wondering if I had already entered the Kingdom of Heaven in Francis Bay- when I was diagnosed with stage-four bladder cancer.

An old college buddy- an eminent cancer researcher- went through the treatment options with me. We were in our early sixties. He had, he claimed, wasted a lifetime's work trying to find a cure for a disease that would never be cured. He had watched too many patients die of cancer.

Jesus, he thought HE had wasted a lifetime's work? I couldn't even go there with him.

I've never seen anyone as afraid of cancer as my friend- the world-class cancer expert.

I'd survived two heart attacks already, and I'd nearly died a violent death so many times I couldn't even count. I wasn't really afraid of dying. I was afraid of... Of what, exactly? Why did I find dying of cancer so terrifying after the kind of life I had led?

I got him to prescribe sufficient pain medication to continue my sailing trip in the Caribbean. Enough medication for the time left.

I couldn't talk Joyce into taking a leave of absence from Fortz and joining me. I didn't want her to know about the cancer. So I didn't play that card.

I talked her into negotiating some extra vacation. But things kept coming up. She'd schedule a trip to sail with me, and then she'd cancel at the last minute...

Nevertheless, I was rarely alone on the boat. Some old college buddies came. Friends from the early days at Fortz.. It's not hard to get people to join you for a free boating trip in the Caribbean, even if you've been as horrible a shit as Francis Bay.

Was it the medication that was making me feel like I was in the Kingdom of Heaven?

I don't think so.

As my friend the world-renowned cancer researcher was painfully learning, much of the point of growing old is coming to terms with your failure and letting go of your dreams. He was a failed crusader against a global cancer epidemic. I am a failed poet. A horribly failed one.

Maybe it doesn't matter any more.

As my insides begin to come apart in a hellish way, I'm thinking about other things now. I've moved on to more pressing matters.

17

I first screwed Luisa in Paris. In a three-star hotel above the Rue De L'Opera. The windows were open and the curtains danced with a chilly spring breeze.

I felt alive and hard and far younger than I was. I felt dirty and dishonest and scheming and awful.

I had, I can assure you, absolutely no intention of falling in love.

By this time, I was a vice-president at Fortz. We lived outside Paris. Or I should say I lived outside of Paris. Joyce, my wife, was a client manager with Fortz working on a long-term project in Bangalore. We saw each other every eight to ten weeks. It had been about three years since our son killed himself. We were making it, but just barely. I don't see how Joyce was surviving the weeks alone in Bangalore. Maybe she was screwing someone, too. I wouldn't be surprised.

Luisa had written to Joyce via email. Joyce forwarded the note to me. This was after the vacation we spent with Luisa and Ford on the Vineyard. Luisa had finished grad school. She was coming to Paris. Could she take us to dinner?

Joyce wasn't going to be in Paris. It would be several weeks before she would be back in France. I took Luisa out to dinner to impress. I failed. Her French was better than mine, although I was slow to pick up on that and had already made a bit of an ass of myself.

She was such a lovely girl. I was such a miserable, wreck of an old man. We had one of those dinners, though, that stretches on and on, with three bottles of wine, and cognac, until the restaurant staff were hanging around waiting for the two of us to leave.

At the beginning of the dinner, one of her father's best and oldest friends was talking with her. By the end of the meal, that same man was a guy who was going to screw her.

You'd think I could draw a boundary somewhere during that transition. You'd think a man as experienced in business and in intelligence could just keep his wits about him. France had about thirty million other women I could have screwed, if that was what I needed. And as many people as I had cynically betrayed in my life's work, you'd think keeping that one old, dear, friendship alive would have made it worth just giving Luisa a peck on the cheek at the door to her hotel.

But it didn't work that way.

She didn't give me a chance. She was going for broke at that point in the evening. For God's sake, I thought, she was almost half my age, and I could have just shown a moment's decency.

There I was passionately embracing her on the Rue de L'Opera. We kept at it for a few minutes, until I invited myself up to her room.

I wasn't going to screw her in Joyce's bed at our apartment. Joyce sure as hell didn't need that, after all we'd been through. After our hearts were ripped out and dragged through the streets of Warsaw in a shrieking ambulance, our son's injuries obviating the need for any real speed. He was just being transported to a hospital for a formal declaration of the obvious: That his parents were the most despicable, failed human beings on the planet.

Maybe that's why I took Ford's daughter upstairs in that hotel. Maybe I just needed to prove to myself how big a shit I really was.

But the enchanting goddess of a girl wouldn't let me get away with it. She made me want to be alive again, as much as I desperately wanted not to be.

Being dead would be so much easier. So much less painful.

18

MICE. That's the acronym we're trained to use for recruiting intelligence assets. It's basic training stuff.

Money, Ideology, Coercion, and Ego.

I still like the child molestation analogy better.

But for the purposes of this analysis, let's run my affair with Luisa through the standard framework.

Money: I was addicted to it. Joyce and I were making a mountain of it. I had my VP's salary at Fortz. She had her client manager's salary. We both had our standard expat packages from Fortz. Housing, moving expenses, cost-of-living-differential-adjustment- all of that was covered before we even got our salaries. Then I had my pay from the agency. I'm guessing the total was close to a million a year. Much of it was tax-free. We got the legal exemption on foreign-earned income from Fortz. And then I got special treatment from the IRS. Because of my work with the agency, if I ever had any trouble with the IRS, for as long as I lived, I had a telephone number I could call to make it all go away.

Still I can't really tell you how much money I netted in a year, or how much we spent. We made a consistent hash of it. We always have. Obviously we spent more than we had coming in, because we were always desperate for cash. That's what made me such a good asset. The special IRS phone number-

face it, that was part of the coercion. Once I had called a couple of times, they had me. They knew I was cheating on my
taxes. All they had to do to have me thrown in jail was make a
call themselves. They never communicated the threat to me.
But I was no dumb ass. They didn't have to shout in my ear.

Then there was the chalet in Switzerland. We loved the
place, a spectacular home in the mountains just above Ver-
bier. The deal was: the agency would use it as a safe house
whenever we weren't there. It was deeded in my name. It was
paid for. I never paid taxes on the "gift." There was no proof
the agency had given it to me. For all any prosecutor or jury
would be able to see, it had been paid for with cash from drug
deals. Or weapons deals. Or you name it. I had the travel
record, the framework on which a prosecution could easily be
hung.

MICE. Money. Ideology. Coercion. Ego.

That covers the money part. And you can see from the discussion above- the coercion part was equally well-covered,
even without my extracurricular sexual activities.

What about ego? They had that one cold.

I always found the ego thing to be just a bit more difficult
to spot in a potential asset than you'd think. The flashy, pre-
varicating bigmouth, you see, often really doesn't have much
of an ego. He's just overcompensating for the dark hole where
his ego ought to be.

It's the quiet, self-assured types that are swinging an ego
between their legs just long enough to trip them.

That was me. Churchill famously said spies required a
"passion for anonymity." Well haven't I always been passionate?

Don't let it mislead you. I spoke eight languages fluently. I
had two master's degrees from Ivy League universities. I
worked out. I watched my weight. Women flirted with me

long before my son's death led me actually to screw around on my wife.

In that Paris restaurant, Luisa gazed at me as if I were James Bond. Hell, I was James Bond. I was well over fifty years old, and this spectacular twenty-something-year-old polyglot was drinking herself silly over me. Talk about ego.

Luisa knew and supposedly "just loved" my wife of twenty-five years. Luisa's mother had come to our wedding carrying Luisa in her womb, for Christ's sake.

Well, there. Take it from me. Ego was covered.

That left ideology.

19

Think about that one for a minute. What exactly does ideology mean?

Two ancient Greek roots. Ideo- meaning form or pattern. -logy from the Greek originally meaning "word." But the root has morphed into the "-logy" suffix in English, which means "the study of."

The study of forms or patterns? What kinds of forms and patterns?

Fractals dancing in the shimmering desert air?

The word "ideology" was invented in the eighteenth century by French philosophers. But it was rarely used until Marx emerged in the turmoil of the Industrial Revolution. At the beginning of the twentieth century, "ideology" had come to mean basically what it means today.

Which is what? The best I could ever determine, ideology means an irrational, prejudicial belief that the believer understands how things really are. Ideology seldom is subject to interference from exposure to actual facts.

Ideology is a rather dogged and particularly dangerous form of telling ourselves fictions.

If we, as well-trained spy recruiters, looked for human beings who were strongly afflicted by a certain ideology, we were basically looking for particularly imaginative fabulists- people who deluded themselves with the most elaborate and elegant of stories- fictions that ordered the chaotic universe in ways that were wrong, but in ways that made them more comfortable.

Well, that made the game easier.

I can tell you, while I still maintain the best spies can smell a potential recruit the way a child molester can smell his prey, I found in actual practice that keeping an eye open for an ideologue was almost equally useful.

You might think because I was recruiting intelligence assets for the United States, I was looking for ideologues who supported the concepts of capitalism and democracy.

You couldn't be more wrong.

I was looking for devoted Marxists.

Later, I was looking for devoted Islamists.

Basically, I was looking for the dope who had bought the enemy's whole agenda with the last remaining balance on his last remaining credit card.

When you find the devoted ideologue, you have found a child with no firm concept of what is right and wrong. In desperation, they grasp the fables some power figure feeds them. They go along with this abuse of power to the point that they base their entire life, their entire sense of self-worth on it.

They are so pathetically vulnerable.

The child molester takes the prey, feeds it kindness and sympathy and seeming love, and then when the horror begins, the child has no rational sense of right and wrong with which to judge the depravity to which they are being subjected. The prey of the child molester comes from some abusive and chaotic background, where the drunken or drugged adults wielded their power in completely arbitrary and bizarre ways, until the child could no longer see the truth, couldn't see the actual benevolence behind the Universe, could not tell what was right or wrong, feel true love, believe what we are all born to believe, or sense what we are all born to sense. The molester himself then becomes the handler, the recruiter and runner of agents, who manipulates this child into doing unimaginably abhorrent things while he or she simply imagines everything is as it should be.

I hope you are beginning to see, now, how a professional recruiter of intelligence assets uses ideology. Find the political or the religious ideologue, and you have found the child who has no attachment to the truth.

I had parroted the official ideological line as I was being recruited into the agency, but I never really believed it. I knew what they wanted to hear from me on the subject of political ideology. So I fed them what they were looking for. The trouble was, deep down inside, where it counted, I was a stickler for the truth.

Maybe this was what Luisa was able to see in me.

Maybe it was what her handlers were able to see.

I think there were complicating factors, also. When I fell prey to Luisa, the predictable disasters and heartbreaks of middle age had laid me bare to the truth. I was a whore to it. I wanted so badly to have communion with it I was willing to do anything, to betray anything, to degrade myself in any way.

I may not have had much experience with the truth. I may not even have been able to see it for myself. But I fantasized, at least, that the truth existed.

Making up lies just wasn't doing it for me any more.

20

Warsaw may have changed that for me.

The operation started with the fall of the Iron Curtain in the early nineties. Under the banner of a blossoming free market, I deployed to the former Warsaw Pact states.

My cover was as manager of a private equity fund designed to invest in real estate development. Those days were the Wild West of real estate development in the former Soviet bloc. Financially desperate former apparatchiks controlled the best real estate and, thus, the best projects. Bribery worked. The least prudent of western developers and lenders rushed in to take advantage of enormous profits to be made. Fifty years of crappy Soviet communism had left slums as bad as the Bronx-inhabited by highly educated, energetic people.

Warsaw was not a city with sections of slums. Warsaw was one, vast, carefully planned slum.

No Soviet building there was worth saving. At the time, anybody who wanted to make money, either by participating in the new capitalist economy or shaking it down with old-fashioned, communist graft and crime, had dough to spend and nowhere decent to live or work.

If a developer could tie up a site and bribe his or her way through the permitting process, he or she could make a fortune.

Few western banks would lend in this wild-west atmosphere. Still fewer equity investors would jump in. It was easy to draw up a business plan. The agency wanted me there, and they were always able to deliver cash when I needed it. Investors and lenders materialized. I was flying to Warsaw every month.

Meanwhile, we were living outside Philadelphia, in Ardmore. My son attended boarding school in New England. He was a troubled teen. But a troubled teen at boarding school is somebody else's trouble for most of every month.

Joyce was still with Fortz, working in their Philadelphia office. I had left Fortz at the instigation of the agency. We framed it as mid-career wanderlust, a way to scratch my entrepreneurial id, but that was just a cover. I could go back to Fortz whenever the agency wanted me back there. I could go anywhere the agency wanted me to go.

I couldn't go anywhere they didn't want me to go.

Now they wanted me in Warsaw.

21

Warsaw. Grenada. For me, there is a truth in these places. I went to Grenada in the aftermath of Reagan's invasion, ostensibly as a Fortz consultant updating the weaponry of the Grenadian National Defense Force.

There was an enchantingly beautiful place in Grenada- a villa that had previously belonged to an English Duke, a supposed Nazi sympathizer. The Grenadians had confiscated the old bugger's villa on one of the most beautiful black sand beaches of the island. I'm sitting in the old villa now, typing this. Nowadays it's a boutique hotel. The first time I saw it was after the invasion. The Grenadian National Defense Force had turned it into a headquarters building. It was a place where Cubans could take the local women to screw and swim at the beach.

One of my Grenadian friends took me there in the months after our invasion. The villa was empty and forlorn then. Evil and lies hung from the mildewed walls and bats hung on the rafters.

But the setting was so beautiful. The black sand beach, the bay, the impossibly green hills on either side. The volcanic, layered rock formations. The insistent trade wind and lapping of the gentle waves on the sand. Large seas breaking on the reef farther out.

I associate my memories of this place with my memories of Warsaw. For this was the first time I became conscious of the inescapable stench of lies and evil in a place.

In Warsaw I could smell the ghetto. The uprising. The Stalin years. The train ride out to Auschwitz.

My own lies. My own mission. My own guilt.

It was just a grinding cycle, and it began to bother me. First it came as a sense of smell, as if a skunk were hiding in my briefcase. Then as a dull pain between my shoulder blades, and later as an ache and a heaviness throughout my body. It built over the months, until I began to behave erratically enough to catch the attention of my handlers.

I really don't want to remember this anymore.

I want the waitress to bring me another dark rum and tonic. I want to sit on the terrace until the sun disappears and I can watch the bats begin to circle towards home.

I'm just trying to be honest, here. This is not something I've gotten to be good at, yet. It's so much easier to tell a smooth, polished lie.

But I don't want to lie anymore.

22

If I'm telling the truth, let's go with the obeah man.

I'm willing to bet this is too much truth for you.

I met him one day as I was hitchhiking across St. John. I had walked across the island from Francis Bay, over the mountains on the east end and down to Skinny Legs' bar in Coral Bay. It was too strenuous a hike for an old man. After a couple of beers and a hamburger, I decided to take the bus back to Cruz Bay rather than attempt those mountain trails again.

Except there was no bus.

Or, as the Dominican woman I found at the bus stop told me, "*Depende. A veces viene, a veces no.*" Sometimes the bus came. Sometimes not.

So I pointed my finger at the ground, the Caribbean way to flag a ride, and the obeah man picked me up.

Prospero was his name. I had to ask him to repeat the name three times before I could understand what he was saying... Prospero. Like the Shakespeare play. Oh, brave new world.

The drive from Coral Bay to Cruz Bay takes twenty to thirty minutes along the mountainous backbone of St. John. Prospero was stoned. His dreadlocks reeked of marijuana smoke, and the whites of his eyes were bright red.

He spoke the deepest West Indian dialect, making almost no effort to code shift into English so I could understand him.

I can't really remember why I started talking about jumbies. Just the spirit of the surrounding forest, I guess.

We were passing through the National Park, near the Reef Bay trail head. We haltingly talked about the forest and hurricane Irma, and how different the island looked now after the storm. For some reason I mentioned jumbies.

Prospero went deeply silent.

For a long, awkward time.

I had enjoyed talking with this stoned Rasta. It made the wild ride a bit less terrifying. I thought we might sideswipe half the oncoming cars or trucks we passed.

"You don't believe in jumbies," I said, laughing.

Nothing but stony, determined silence.

"I'm sorry," I said, after a long, awkward pause. "I apologize if I said something inappropriate."

"Not me," Prospero said. "Ask him he mind."

And there in the back seat was a man who had not been there before.

This is the truth.

I was overwhelmed with a sensation of fear. Cold, sharp fear, a fear such as I had never felt in my life.

He was a young, black man with close-cropped hair. A slightly-built guy in nothing but flimsy, dark-colored shorts. Or was he wearing a loin cloth?

He smiled directly at me. He had no teeth. His smile was a hideous black hole, infinitely deep.

Then he reached out and touched my cheek.

His touch was like a soldering iron.

I screamed and jerked away, slamming my head against the windshield. The young man disappeared.

"Watch what you say," Prospero said. "You too close on the truth."

"Jesus!" I screamed.

"What?" Prospero said. "You want him too?"

23

Have you heard of St. John's slave rebellion? It took place when Denmark owned St. John in the eighteenth century.

The Danish Virgin Islands were host to one of the most brutal slave experiences in the New World. This is sort of like saying Donald Trump was one of the most outrageous philanderers ever to become an American president. That is to say, the Virgin Islands were simply the worst of a very unsavory lot.

The climate in St. John was difficult and dangerous. The work was grueling. Disease was rampant, the management spectacularly venal and inept. Life expectancy for newly imported slaves was less than seven years.

The sugar industry was so profitable for plantation owners that- back in Copenhagen- Virgin Island landholders were barred from having carriages and palaces more lavish than the Danish king's- to save the king from embarrassment.

The St. John slave rebellion quickly fermented in this tropical hell. But it first began growing far away, in Africa.

Slavery existed in Africa long before the Portuguese started importing African slaves to the Americas. Africans had been enslaved by other Africans and traded among African tribes since... who knows?

When Europeans began buying African slaves in the sixteenth century, the long-thriving African slave trade simply turned toward the sea. Tribes traded slaves until the slaves arrived at a seaport to be sold to Europeans. By the height of the Transatlantic trade in the eighteenth century, the African tribes who controlled these ports had grown enormously wealthy and powerful.

Power and wealth attract envy, and it was not unknown for neighboring African kingdoms to attack and overthrow those who controlled the lucrative slaving seaports.

The rebellion on St. John had its genesis in one of these wars. A group of slaves arrived on St. John who had previously been nobles in one of the very wealthy tribes who controlled a seaport. These former nobles had been attacked, overthrown, and enslaved by their conquerors. Within a few weeks, the vanquished rulers found themselves in hellish conditions on that most beautiful of twenty-first century tourist destinations. In fact, they found themselves enslaved in hellish conditions on the very shores of Francis Bay.

The leaders of St. John's slave rebellion, truth be told, had no interest whatsoever in liberating their fellow Africans. They simply wanted to kill the white managers of the plantations, take over the plantations for themselves, and grow rich off the work of the other Africans.

You could say they underestimated the ferocious racism of their European neighbors. But I doubt they did. They probably raged with an equally ferocious racism, tribalism, greed, cruelty, and barbarity. Maybe they raged with more of those emotions than the Europeans.

After the rebels had killed or run off most of the Europeans on St. John, and after they had managed to hold on to power as the new owners of the island for several months, a European military force routed them and hunted their survivors throughout the island. The whites captured and brutally killed every single one of the rebels within a year.

There is little that is romantic in the story. It is a proud story among the descendants of enslaved Africans who make up the majority of the U. S. Virgin Islands' inhabitants today. But it's a proud story because their guys stuck it to the man. Not because the rebels fought for truth, justice, and the American way.

Oh, bugger, they probably did fight for the American way, but...

24

My cancer was diagnosed in Grenada.

This is how it really happened.

My buddy, the cancer researcher from Sloan Kettering, was spending three days and three nights with me on my boat in Francis Bay. We had intended to sail to Gorda Sound, but the wind was ferocious, as it often is in January.

So we stayed in Francis Bay. Every night, we took a taxi to Cruz Bay to eat at a restaurant. I guess my buddy didn't like the meals I cooked on board. He paid for the taxi and the dinners, and that was how I met Prospero.

(So... yes, my previous story about meeting Prospero was a variation on the truth. But I'm writing a novel here. What do you expect?)

Prospero (not his real name) was from Dominica. The real Prospero was a taxi driver with a ramshackle Suzuki SUV. We got his telephone number from the taxi stand in Cruz Bay. None of the regular drivers wanted to run as far from town as Maho Bay after dark. Prospero made a business of running people around the island in the dark- the more remote the destination and the darker the night the better. And the higher the fare.

This was also, by the way, the first time I thought I saw a jumbie. It's just not as dramatic as the later story, still mostly true, when one burned my cheek.

So, this time, we were riding back to Francis Bay in Prospero's taxi.

The windows were open. My buddy and I were drunk. We could hear coquis pinging in the forest we were rushing through.

As we drove by Jumbie Beach, I pointed at the roadside sign and said to my friend, "Hey John, do you know what jumbies are?"

Prospero went silent. I could see in the rearview mirror he had a large grin.

There followed some drunken conversation about jumbies, in which I explained the mystery to my scientist buddy.

"Isn't that right?" I said to Prospero.

"I don't know," Prospero said, laughing.

"Oh, come on," I said. "You're from Dominica and you don't know anything about jumbies?"

Prospero just laughed.

"You see," I said to my scientist friend. "Jumbies."

And then, for just a moment, I thought I saw another person sitting in the front seat of the car. It was an old, white man, wearing a faded bathing suit.

The sensation went away almost immediately.

I was too drunk, and it was too dark, and the coquis were too loud, and the scent of bay trees was too strong, and I just couldn't hold on to what I had seen long enough to really believe it.

I went silent.

Prospero laughed.

We rode to Maho Bay without talking any more about the supernatural.

The next day I told my buddy about the blood in my urine and the pain in my back. He consulted via cell phone with a colleague in New York. They arranged for a former fellow of theirs at St. George's medical school in Grenada to perform a cystoscopy and send the results to Sloan Kettering.

I just needed to sail down to Grenada.

Just! Hah!

It was a tough, one-week trip. I was trying to hide the whole reason from Joyce. I invited her to fly down for a week in Grenada at a beautiful boutique hotel on a black sand beach.

It was the former Caribbean residence of a British lord. We made it a week together. Just barely.

The week after my wife left, I underwent a biopsy. Follow-up imaging showed cancer that had spread throughout much of my torso.

This was not an easy truth to believe.

25

At one point in my psychiatric counseling, I was asked to recount my earliest childhood memories.

I remembered going with my grandfather to a small office behind his house. The office contained a wooden desk, a chair, and a refrigerator. Pops kept six-ounce bottles of Coca-Cola in that refrigerator. When we went to the office, he would open a Coke for me.

He was a bank president when I was a young child. When I told this story to my therapist, I attributed that early retained memory to my thrill at getting the Coca-Cola and getting to spend time with my grandfather in his special office.

But the therapist wouldn't let me dwell in this neat fiction. She made me dig deeper. In all likelihood, she claimed, the memory had been fixed in my mind by some terribly painful scene I could no longer remember. Was there any way I could imagine what the truth behind the memory was?

Well, with a bit of recollection, I was able to concoct a story that met her requirements. Now that I think back on it, I was just concocting. I had no firm memory of this concocted story. I just remembered my grandfather, his home office behind the garage, his desk and chair, the refrigerator, and the Coca Colas. Those memories are vivid. They are the truth. I think.

Here is the story my therapist led me to concoct:

We were living with my grandparents because my father had left. My mother had taken me to live with her parents because she no longer had enough income to stay in our home.

My grandfather, I learned rather late in life, was a terrible alcoholic.

My mother, a young woman of twenty-four, had been plunged back into the chaotic home she thought she had escaped by going to college and finding a husband. Now she was a single mother with little income.

I think it is safe to concoct a story, then, from these fragments told by my mother (although I admit it is sheer folly to accept stories told by my mother as the truth. The stories themselves change radically over the decades, as she begins to believe the lies she tells herself.)

Anyway, here's the story my therapist had me concoct:

My grandfather kept his bourbon out in that home office. It was in the wooden desk. I even began to reconstruct some memories of his retrieving the bourbon bottle from the drawer. I was his trusted, esteemed companion, as he escaped from his nagging wife and neurotic daughter, escaped from the drudgery of being the bank president in a small Southern mill town, and took his favorite grandson out to play. Ecstatic with release, he slid into a stately, drunken stupor in his banker's suit.

Surely I enjoyed this as a little kid. I got my Coke. He got his happy drink. He was jolly and he loved me so, and then, I imagine...

We were discovered.

My grandmother, whom I remember mostly as an unhappy shrew (although I have been told by those who knew her she was entirely the opposite) would have been furious at my drunken grandfather. Perhaps she was furious at me for being an accomplice. She would have screamed. She would have thrown dishes. (An old neighbor of hers once told me she did this.) My mother would have been icy and furious and brutal in her rejection of my grandfather- and, surely with me. She never threw dishes. She never shouted. But God could she make you feel like shit.

Once I concocted this story about my early childhood, my therapist was very proud of me. I had done the detective work to uncover the truth that was driving my own aberrant behavior. I felt better.

The truth had been discovered. I was cured.

26

St. John.

You have the drugged-up young people working their beach jobs, waiting tables, tending bar, crewing day boats.

You have the wizened, middle-aged dropouts who have drifted away from their crumbling lives all over the world.

You have the duplicitous and the marginally criminal, like me, who have found a way to scramble ashore and cling for a while.

And you have the abidingly mysterious, like Prospero.

After I had leaped from his car in Cruz Bay that afternoon the jumbie burned me, after I had drowned my fear in half a dozen rum punches at the Longboard, after I had returned to my life tied to a mooring ball in Francis Bay- I kept running into him.

His rusted, dilapidated Suzuki Sidekick would come barreling around a curve. I could see his dreadlocks flying in the breeze. I smelled pot smoke as he raced past.

He was smiling- directly at me.

When I saw him, I had the same panicked feeling. The spot on my cheek burned.

I sailed away to Vieques for a couple of weeks to try to get away from my panic. But that was no good. Anchored on the south side of the island, I just got the creeps. I couldn't sleep.

Even here, in this Puerto Rican island with an entirely different culture, my imagination was wild with jumbies. At night, as they howled past on the trade winds, I huddled sleeplessly in my berth, clutching knees to my chest.

After two weeks and nearly a case of Don Q Gold rum, I bashed back upwind to St. John and picked up a mooring in Francis Bay.

Old, so-called friends were scheduled to visit. I thought I would be o.k. with company on board. I thought I could regain my grip on the great lie I imagined was life.

But I had had too much truth by that time to fully return to the life of the living. I had already begun to slip away into the universe of the dead, the realm of the ultimate, inescapable truth I had been hiding from all along.

27

After my return from Vieques, my so-called friends came to visit on the boat, and we did a lot of drinking.

We were in St. Croix, one night, anchored off Christiansted, talking about books we had read recently.

I had just finished *Lincoln in the Bardo* and was tremendously impressed.

To explain this admiration to my friends, I recounted a scene in the novel where one of the characters goes to some ethereal place after his death. A group of supernatural beings is interviewing the newly dead. When some of the dead are interviewed (they're not really interviewed- it's more like their lives are examined in some ethereal way) at any rate, when some of the dead are examined, a spectacularly beautiful vista of brilliant, mountainous diamonds- glistening fractals- opens up. The departed pass on to this marvelous realm that Saunders manages to make pull at the reader's emotions like---

Well, it pulls at you in a very familiar and very profound way. At least it pulled at me like that.

But some of the dead have a different result. As their lives are examined, the angelic creatures begin to scowl. Then the examiners begin to vomit. They all vomit like cannons. Well, maybe not like cannons, but....

Then the newly dead are cast into this....

It's like the darkness where there is wailing and gnashing of teeth.

I've always been so fucking terrified of that place.

Anyway. I was drunk. My friends were drunk. We had gotten thrown out of the last bar we visited on St. Croix. I was telling them about this passage from Saunders' weird novel. Only I couldn't get it all across to them.

I started crying.

I don't know why I started crying.

"I don't know why I'm doing this," I sputtered to my two drunk friends.

The next morning, I woke up sprawled across the cockpit bench seats, my ass drooping to the cockpit sole. My head and shoulders were on one seat. My feet were on the opposite seat. I felt like death.

I don't know how I had stayed there all night.

I don't know why I'm telling this story.

28

Here's something more interesting, if perhaps even less relevant.

When I began having an affair with Luisa, a woman a quarter of a century younger than I, I could still get an erection.

But that didn't last long.

By the time of our second tryst, a weekend near Brittany's Cap Frehel, I had begun to experience what would be my inescapable future.

I had previously endured an episode or two of impotence at home with Joyce. We had been married a long time by then. We laughed it off. I can't remember if these episodes began exactly after I had begun screwing Luisa...

Truth, Franny. Stop and search for the truth.

The first night I took Luisa to that small inn in Brittany, we had a romantic fireside dinner, a spectacular meal of roast lamb and too much wine. The wine didn't hinder me. She was radiant, drunk herself and grinning like a kid at Christmas.

I screwed her for hours that night. I had never in my life been able to perform with such endurance.

Luisa was a screamer. She moaned and called on the Lord for what seemed like two or three hours. (Surely it was less?)

The next morning, at breakfast, in the same dining room as the night before, she was a radiantly beautiful girl who looked like she had screwed all night. I looked like... God only knows. I looked like a serial killer. Everyone else in the place looked at me as if I was. I grinned like an idiot during the whole meal. I remember feeling like a man half my age.

That day, I walked and necked with Luisa on the pink cliffs at Cap Frehel. The sun was brilliant. The sea was whipped into whitecaps. We cooed and nuzzled like teenagers.

That night, I took her to a restaurant in the village to avoid the glares of the innkeepers and their other guests. Again, we drank heavily. I drove back to the inn in the darkness, anticipating another romp in the sack.

I had to ask the innkeeper for the key at the desk. He scowled at me like I was a child molester.

When we got to the room, I was absolutely, irreconcilably flaccid.

No amount of stimulation could change things. Luisa tried until she laughed. Then she laughed until she cried.

I cried, too. I can't really say why we were crying. It's not like conversation led to the tears, and it's not like our laughter led to the tears. We cried over what we knew was the truth.

The next day we drove back to Paris and didn't talk about it at all.

29

The affair continued in Paris. Luisa would go away and travel around Europe for a week or two. Then she would come back to town and we would screw. Well, it was more than that. Half the time I couldn't technically screw.

When we couldn't make love, we talked. This was a kind of romantic encounter I never really experienced before. We sat and gabbed, on a non-sexual basis, often quite naked, sometimes quite drunk, in her shabby hotel room.

I didn't want to take her home to Joyce's bed.

When we talked, we were much more like who we really were. I was one of her father's oldest friends. She was my old friend's daughter. Only we were naked. And we knew how bad we were being.

This was fun. I thought at the time it was doubly fun for me because I was an intelligence operative.

I didn't yet realize that it was just as fun for her for exactly the same reason.

The nakedness and the impotence were stimulants. It was like the best of intelligence work. One developed these relationships based on trust and friendship and betrayal and desperation and profound confidence and blatant deceit. Intelligence work is like being in love, really, except that I made it a personal rule never to have sex with my assets. Apparently

Luisa had sex with hers.

When they could get it up.

The rest of the time we just shared our catty, jaded views of the world. Neither of us believed our compatriots' patriotic bullshit. Neither of us believed (at least as far as Luisa let on) the patriotic bullshit of any country. We shared a snide, good-humored view of the world and its inhabitants. This was a secret shared openly in our seedy hotel, the slightly overweight old man and the decidedly lithe, naked beauty.

We talked and drank and sat with legs akimbo across the room from each other, delightfully in love.

Luisa would come to me and sit naked in my lap. We would neck like teenagers.

Sometimes this would revive the manhood in me. Sometimes it was just different, and oh so unexpectedly wonderful.

Paris was loud outside in the street.

I was limp and in love indoors.

The truth... Oh who the hell knew what the truth was in those long, delicious moments?

30

I was coming off the ferry one day in Cruz Bay, having crossed from St. Thomas after picking up some fuel filters, when I ran into Prospero again.

Literally.

I was walking sideways, looking toward the safari taxis, wondering who would give me a lift back out to Francis Bay, when I collided with Prospero.

When I saw him, I screamed.

Everybody in Cruz Bay seemed to stop and stare at me.

Prospero laughed a belly laugh.

He took my elbow and began to lead me.

"Come with me, my brother," he said. He pulled me off to the beach in front of the bars. Most of the buildings along that strip of beach were still in ruins after the hurricane. The sea grape trees were full of leaves again, shading the sand from the afternoon sun.

Prospero pulled an enormous spliff from his pocket.

"What the fuck are you doing, man?" I said. There were cops standing by the ferry dock.

"They don't bother me," Prospero said.

I gawked at the cops. They were already watching us. Prospero kept guiding me farther afield. He lit his spliff and took a voluminous hit, his red eyes gleaming at me. He offered the spliff and blew a thunderhead of smoke.

"Fuck it," I said. I took the spliff and smoked, too.

The cops were laughing.

"Yeh," Prospero said, "You ain't got to worry bout them fools. You got jumbie problems, my brother."

He laughed and pulled me to sit on a ruined foundation in the shade.

"Who the hell are you, man?" I said.

Prospero sucked a huge toke of smoke from the spliff and smiled.

"You have no idea," he said.

He giggled, sort of. Smoke leaked from his nostrils and between his teeth. Was it coming out of his ears?

"Hey," he said. "Don't nobody just find me, you know."

"I just *found* you?" I said.

"What the fuck you think happened?" he said.

I growled in exasperation. Prospero passed the spliff to me. I smoked because I couldn't find anything to say.

"That thing touch you in the car," he said. "Don't touch no-body. "

"I feel so honored."

"He standing right there. Behind you," Prospero said.

I wheeled. There was nothing but air. And sand. And a ruined beach bar.

"What we gonna do with you, Francis Bay?" Prospero said.

I had never told the man my name.

31

Remember my first description of Francis Bay? The setting I claimed is the most lovely on the planet? Remember Whistling Cay, the remote island guarding the mouth of the bay, where a ruined customs house seems to have Obeah artifacts posed around it on the stone beach? It is separated from the mainland of St. John by a narrow stretch of water- so narrow a person could swim across it, if that person were a strong swimmer and was careful of the tidal currents.

Across that narrow strip of water is Mary's Point, a high headland on St. John, with red cliffs running down to the beautiful sea below.

The St. John's slave uprising, according to local lore, ended here, when the final twelve rebels, having held out for nearly a year against the Europeans, jumped to their death from those cliffs rather than be captured by a French military force that was mopping up the final slave resistance in 1734.

Not all these details of the St. John slave uprising quite match the details I've shared with you, I realize. I've grossly oversimplified my telling of the slave uprising of 1733-1734 in St. John.

Like all stories, it begs for oversimplification. It begs to be condensed, to be cleaned up, to be contextualized.

For almost four hundred years, people have been telling this story, spinning it for their own political and historical purposes, just making it a cool ghost story, maybe making it a story of black strength and indomitable spirit in the face of barbaric white suppression.

Or making it a story of white strength and indomitable spirit in the face of barbaric black treachery.

But it's a bloody, complex thing to try to get a grip on.

First, there's the paucity of actual, historical evidence.

Do a bit of research, and you'll find the most complete, the most readable, and the most influential story of the rebellion is, in fact, a novel- a work of fiction entitled *Night of the Silent Drums,* written by John L. Anderson, otherwise known as Lonzo Anderson, and published by Scribners in 1975. The book has long been out of print and, as of this writing, has an Amazon Best Sellers Ranking of #1,230,658.

There is also the story of the slave rebellion in *St. John, Off the Beaten Track,* written and apparently self-published by Gerald Singer in 1996.

In terms of scholarly work, one can readily find on the Internet, as of the time of this writing, an unpublished Ph. D. dissertation by Dr. H. K. Norton of Syracuse University from 2013 entitled *The Landscape of the St. John Slave Rebellion.* While this treatise may be unpublished, it is, as of this writing, posted in full by Syracuse University on the Internet.

Dr. Norton acknowledges her reliance on the *Silent Drums* novel and local lore as she lays out her story of the rebellion. But she is an Anthropologist, which, if it doesn't make her an actual scientist, makes her an actual social scientist. She will use scientific methods to find the truth, or at least some more comfortable version of the truth, one hopes, in this very old story.

Dr. Norton does, thankfully, translate and quote a number of primary historical reports about the rebellion for us. And she relies extensively on recent archaeological exploration by herself and others, largely made possible because many sites of the rebellion now lie within the Virgin Islands National Park.

Dr. Norton's story is far more detailed and more scientific than the neat little story I have told you about the rebellion. I could pick out some details of her story- the fact that the rebels were Akwamu nobles, that there were relatively few of them, that many of the other African slaves on the island joined in the fight against them. I could tell you where the rebellion started (Fort Fredricksvaern in Coral Bay), where many of the major engagements took place (a good many in the area of what are now called Caneel Bay and Cinnamon Bay), even where some of the final engagements took place.

I could tell you the names of some of the Akwamu nobles who were leaders of the rebellion. My favorite is a woman, who the Europeans thought was a man, but whose corpse revealed her to be a woman when she was discovered near what is now known as Brown's Bay in a very remote part of the park. She was one of two dozen rebels who died in a mass suicide. Her name was Bressu. Or Beaussu. Or something like that. People can't seem to get her name straight.

And they can't seem to get it straight whether this is the storied suicide that ended the rebellion, or whether there was a later suicide, the one everybody's talked about for four hundred years, several miles away at the cliffs on Mary's Point, the cliffs whose bright red rocks, according to local lore, were stained by the blood of the martyred rebel leaders.

Dr. Hopkins herself can't seem to straighten out this part of the story, as admirably scientific and documented and mapped and footnoted as her study is.

We're left, then, with one of the most beautiful places on Earth. There we have a distant, long-ago story of Africans and silent drums. And we have red rock cliffs. You can see them for yourself.

Right across from the cliffs, you can see for yourself the strange little island with the stone beach where the man you call Francis Bay will soon disappear into the black maw of the underbrush on a moonlight night, being led by a jumbie in a loincloth.

32

Now, even though I couldn't see the jumbie behind me, my comprehension of the spirits conjured by Prospero was nearly complete.

I saw nothing. I knew something was there.

Or I almost knew it.

I felt the most incredible anxiety begin to overtake me. It was similar to times in my agency work when I thought I might be killed or imprisoned, when I could see no way out.

"How you staring right at the jumbie and you ain't see it?" Prospero said.

"Fuck you," I said.

A cold sensation, cold like frostbite, swept across the right side of my face and my ear.

"Francis Bay," Prospero said, "you ain't able to see reality."

"And how the hell do you know my name?" I said

Prospero laughed and held the joint out to me again,"You want some more, Mr. Francis?" he said, mocking me.

I was already too stoned to smoke any more. Through my intense intoxication, I told myself he was just naming me based on my usual location, in the way West Indians toy with anybody's name as they get to know them.

"What you doing in St. John?" Prospero said to me.

"I... I don't know," I stammered. I really didn't know. Joyce had thrown me out six months earlier. I had moved onto the boat, thinking she might have me back after a while. She always had before. Then I sailed single-handed down from the Chesapeake, eleven days of sheer terror and exhaustion, slamming into the prevailing winds and waves day and night, fighting against equipment failure and calamity. Fighting against the urge to slip myself off the transom into the boundless darkness every night. Until the spectacular islets and peaks surrounding Francis Bay had materialized out of the haze early one morning.

"You were brought here," Prospero said. "You ain't had no choice, Francis Bay."

I shrugged.

"You an evil man, ain't you?" he said. It wasn't a question. It was a statement of fact. As if it were obvious to anyone.

And I started to cry. I was so stoned, I couldn't control myself. I stood there stoned on the beach in that sugary sand, where half the people at the Cruz Bay ferry terminal could see me, and I sobbed.

Prospero just turned and walked away. He headed off to the south end of the little beach, and he slipped away onto the roadway. He disappeared into the bright, tropical daylight.

So I stood, stoned, trying to catch my breath, wiping the tears and snot from my face. I looked like a drunk bum on the beach in St. John. Not that there weren't plenty of those guys here. I just hadn't ever planned on being one.

I had six or seven Zacapa rums at a bar up beside the roadway. Then I stumbled in darkness back along the beach. In the main square, I found a taxi driver I knew by sight who agreed to drive me back to Maho Bay for twice the normal fare.

I gave him a hug.

He recoiled.

God only knows how I got in the dinghy and climbed aboard my boat in the darkness.

I didn't even put on the latex gloves I kept in my pocket in case of nerve gas agent.

I woke up the next morning sprawled in the cockpit.

Jesus. The sun was bright. How could it be so fucking bright?

I would have jumped in the water to feel better, but I thought I might throw up. Or drown myself.

Once again, for some reason completely incomprehensible to me, I didn't.

33

Eric.

My son.

There, I said it.

I find it so terribly difficult to say his name now. I never talk about him. After I killed Luisa, I stopped talking about Eric altogether. But I rarely spoke of him before that. Joyce and I moved around enough in our life of outrageous lies that we didn't really run into people close enough to have known Eric. It was almost as if he never existed.

Joyce would occasionally mention him, but by that time, our relationship had become so utterly broken she could see by my reaction that mentioning Eric... there, I said his damn name again...

I suffocated Luisa with a pillow. In a hotel room in Lima. There was no way around it. I was going to be eliminated myself if I didn't put a stop to her. But I was probably going to be eliminated anyway.

Luisa knew what she had gotten into. She had always known. She perfectly fucking well knew, I have always told myself.

Eric. There damn it, I'm making myself say it again. Eric had no idea what he was getting into. He just popped out into the world as the most innocent, wide-eyed little wonder. I had no idea a child wet from the birth canal could have a fully-formed personality. I instantly knew this child. The personality he displayed in that first moment would be the personality he carried through life.

I don't know how I got those words out onto the page. And I'm not really sure why I got them out.

34

I told Eric the truth the day he died.

I told him he was a drugged-up little faggot. I told him I knew he sucked other guys' dicks for drugs.

I knew, of course, because the agency made it their business to know. I was too important an asset to have my teenage son wandering through Berlin's night life as a closeted homosexual, prostituting himself for the next dose of heroin. They had to find out what I was exposed to, and they had to share that truth with me.

I had spent enough time in my line of work to know what people are like when their lies and their truth start to crystallize.

I took Eric with me on a trip to Warsaw. Told him I wanted to take him to visit Auschwitz. Like a teenager wants to visit Auschwitz. Like anyone wants to visit Auschwitz.

But we all need to go, don't we?

When I had had my guts ripped out by a fucking agency briefing on my son's heroin addiction and male prostitution, why did I decide to take the poor kid on a trip to Auschwitz?

We never made it there.

We just checked into the Hilton in Warsaw. I ordered as fancy a meal as I could in the restaurant downstairs for dinner. I pounded back Scotch until I had the courage, or the cowardice, to tell him the truth I had learned about him. Right there. Right in the middle of the restaurant, in full view of a hundred strangers. Not that they could hear was I was saying.

But they could see Eric turn ashen white and begin to shake. They could see my little boy begin to sob. They could see... I could see the little child that had emerged from his mother and looked directly at me with that same expression of vulnerability and guileless love, that vain hope that I might be something worthwhile, that I might be a man worth loving, really. That I might be...

Why did I can him a faggot? Where in God's name did that come from?

I reached across the table to hold his hand, but he snatched it away.

As if I were a cobra.

The glasses on our table shattered in a dance of diamonds.

I've often wondered why he was the one who killed himself.

Surely it was supposed to be me. He couldn't have hurt as much as I did.

I was afraid for myself. If I didn't get this mess under control, the agency could drop me. If they dropped me, Fortz was under no obligation to continue to rehire me. Would they even keep Joyce on?

I was scared for Eric. Of course I was scared for Eric and wanted to save him. But there was a certain detachment to my fear. There was that...

Well, it surely came from my relationship with my mother. I had dealt with an addicted loved one before. I knew the ropes. I had already begun to let go of Eric, truth be told.

But I wasn't telling the truth very much in those days. I was lying to myself that Joyce and I had actually been good parents, that I had not drunkenly haunted my son's adolescence, shut up every evening in my bedroom like my mother. Stumbling forth to root about in the unused kitchen, rattling through the ice bin. Dropping cubes into my glass, as the crystalline sound bounced off that tile floor, bouncing, bouncing. Dancing. The tinkling carried my mother farther and farther away, as she floated in the mayonnaise jars full of vodka she managed to hide from me in yet another obscure cupboard. I searched the house like the good secret agent I already was, guessing her every move. She hid. I found. I poured out. She hid even more. I could never keep up. I couldn't get rid of the vodka.

Now my son was sitting across from me in an expensive Warsaw restaurant, breaking glasses, ruining my life. Evading my desperate attempts to fix the situation.

I had to fix it. I had to get it under control.

I could not let the past repeat.

I had to call him a faggot.

I had to call her a bitch. She kissed me right on the mouth. She slipped her tongue in, damn it. I was fourteen years old. I can taste the vodka and the lipstick.

I want to break every fucking glass in Warsaw.

I want to shatter every glass window on every story of the Warsaw Hilton. I want it all to shower down in the fucking icy night.

I want to break through the lies and tell the truth, but the truth is so deadly I can't.

I told it once, right there to Eric.

And look what the hell that did.

The truth may not be any fucking good at all.

Lies can be managed. Lies can be honed. Lies can be hidden away to intoxicate you when you need them the most. Lies are what we all need to hold on to life.

Face the truth, and...

Lose the whole world.

Banish not Jack Falstaff. Banish Jack, and you....

Banish not Francis Bay. Banish Francis...

Perhaps that was just inevitable.

Prospero was right. I was brought to Francis Bay. Francis Bay had to go to that one eponymous rendezvous with death and with life. It was inevitable.

How could I begin to tell you, in some way that you might understand?

I'm going through the easy parts now. The parts that are believable.

When I get to the unbelievable, will you stay with me? Or will you, too, want to launch yourself through a tenth story window of the Warsaw Hilton, following that desk chair into the dark, icy void just outside, seeking the only way out any of us ever really has?

35

Here's a poem for you:

Redhead

by Francis Bay

Gotta Kiss?
You shake your head.
Gotta eskimo?
You shake your head.
Gotta hug?
You shake your head.
I pout.
How bout one big kiss?
Then you smile that devil-eyed smile
And wrap your arms around my neck
And press your little lips on mine
And you look at me
With "ain't that something else?"
In your devilish, angel-blue eyes.

O.k. I was a failure as a poet. But I was a bigger failure as a father. That's my son, by the way. Not my mistress.

I'd like to think I was not really as bad a father, perhaps, as the Francis Bay who is coming out in this novel.

It's far easier to make up a story than to write about the truth.

Reality sucks so.

It makes me just want to have about ten Zacapa rum drinks and go back to my boat.

I can't keep doing that forever.

Here. I'm leafing through the notebook. This is another poem about Eric. I'm going to type this one out for you. When I get through, I'm going for a fucking swim with the turtles.

A Child Pointing at a Puddle

by ...

Brown leaves blown against everything
Twirl, drift, and spin towards the water
In the puddles. "This?" you ask,
Leaving out the what's.
"Leaves."

A long, long time. So much has been here
A long, long time, and will be gone.
Imagine you as my grandfather-
So old he terrifies you, barely able to speak,
For this section of his passage
Seated in his nursing home chair.
His skin is childlike, now.
He puckers his lips like you,
Trying to have you kiss him.
You are scared. You hug me.
I will kiss him for you.

What is there to be afraid of?
There is too much not to be afraid of.
Watch the many colored layers of dawn,
Motionless for all the moment that you see them,
And changing every time you look again
Until the day has come, and what you thought
Was beautiful is gone, replaced by miracles
So numerous you are lost among them.

"This?" you say,
Leaving out the "what's"-
A child's clearer questioning,
Seeking not an explanation
But the word-
A co-conspirator in wonder.

36

The early years with Joyce were like the early months with Luisa.

It disgusts me to hear myself say that, now. I killed Luisa. I might as well have killed Joyce. I killed her son. I could just as well have held the pillow over Joyce's face, too, as she struggled and kicked and ripped my forearms with her fingernails.

It's not easy to kill someone you love.

But we all work at it every day, don't we?

Joyce and I met on a Fortz project in Saudi Arabia. She wasn't living in-country. A single woman engineer couldn't live in-country in Saudi Arabia. She was working in Fortz's office in London. I flew there every month to coordinate with her.

After our first business meeting, I took her out for a pint down the street. Pubs were filled with men and cigarette smoke back in those days. Joyce downed three pints, keeping up with me, and then, without much ado, she accompanied me to my hotel room.

It was the kind of one-night stand, I thought, that would never lead anywhere. But there was an honesty to it, an honesty on Joyce's part, that intrigued me.

The same thing happened with Luisa all those years later.

There was no problem with impotence back when Joyce and I met. There was the occasional problem with premature ejaculation, but Joyce quickly taught me to be a better lover. I had never been with a woman who seemed concerned with her climax. At least I had never been with a woman who was honest enough to let me know it.

I was an idiot. I was a money-running idiot already being groomed by older men at Fortz to be a thug. My previous sexual experiences, no more than a few dozen, were the awkward gropings of a clueless boy, fueled by booze- buried in an impenetrable fog of shame and awkwardness and deceit. I had no idea how to make the act pleasurable to a woman. I had been trained by Penthouse magazine and early porn movies on sixteen-millimeter projectors at bachelor parties.

Joyce was having nothing of it. She let me know what made it good for her, and she made me do it.

Our affair turned into a regular monthly fling- every time I flew to London for the remainder of that project. Within less than a year, I had been transferred to Amsterdam, and we were seeing each other every other weekend.

Joyce was so different from my mother.

Joyce told me the truth. Joyce told everyone the truth- as far as I could tell. She expected other people to tell it to her, and she knew when they didn't. She could navigate comfortably within the realm of naked reality.

When she first told me she loved me, lying in a bed in my Amsterdam flat, she was telling the truth, the whole truth, and nothing but the truth, I now believe. But I couldn't believe her then. How could anyone love me?

My mother had told me she loved me. She told me that hideous lie over and over, reeking of vodka and lipstick, until she convinced me that no one on earth could truthfully tell another person they loved them.

37

The obeah man's magic is African pagan religion transplanted into the New World- fertilized with bondage and cruelty, watered with ignorance and superstition, starved of hope, tempted with Christianity, salved with hypocrisy, pruned by hurricanes, harvested into the overwhelming tropical abundance of life itself.

I've told you the story of the jumbie in Prospero's car. That really happened to me. It was a real to me as the book you are holding in your hand.

Here is the story of the next magic Prospero performed for me.

You need a bit of background here. The day before this encounter with Prospero, I was in Cruz Bay, and I convinced myself I recognized two Russian agents.

Not that I knew them. I just bloody well knew the type. The clothes. The borderline obesity. The haircuts. If I had gotten close enough, I guarantee I could have smelled it on them. Lousy cologne. Last night's vodka.

I caught one of them looking right at me. Amateur move. They recognized their slip-up, and they tried to disappear.

Rather than lead them back to Francis Bay, I hitchhiked all the way across the island to Coral Bay. Had a couple of beers and a burger at Skinny Legs' bar. I may have lost my imagined

Russians when I hitchhiked across the island, but those guys can be skillful.

So I stole a dinghy behind Skinny Legs', drove it out to a boat in Coral Bay that seemed to be unoccupied, and went aboard as if it were mine. I spent much of the afternoon lying in the cockpit. When enough time had passed (how does one ever know when enough time has passed?) I steered the dinghy around the ruins of Fort Fredricksvaern and left it on a beach in Hurricane Hole. I hiked the whole bloody trail over the mountains back to Francis Bay. It was well after dark when I got back aboard my own boat.

The next morning, I found Prospero walking on the beach in Francis Bay. I had gone ashore to deposit a bag of trash in the Park Service bins. It was early morning. No one else was on the beach. I don't think there were any other boats on the moorings that day. Maybe a couple of boats over in Maho Bay just to the south. I can't clearly remember.

So there I was, by myself on one of the most beautiful beaches on earth. I dragged the dinghy only partly out of the water. I threw an anchor a few feet up the beach, grabbed the plastic bag of trash, and headed toward the parking area.

Prospero emerged from the trees in front of me.

It shouldn't have been surprising to find another person on this beach. This was, after all, a public beach in the United States National Park system. But you've heard how my previous day had gone. Prospero's sudden appearance shocked me.

He was naked. Just dreadlocks and jet black skin. His supernatural smile. And his penis swaying as he strolled toward me.

"Francis Bay," he said.

I hurried toward the trash bins.

"Take me to your boat," he said.

I stopped. I dropped the garbage bag.

"What the fuck?" I said. "You're standing there with your dick out, man!"

"It ain't nothing to be afraid of," he said. "Take me to your boat."

He held forth his open hands and displayed two spliffs wrapped in kraft paper.

"I ain't got no lighter, man," he said, laughing. "Ain't got no pockets."

"How the fuck did you get out here?" I said.

"Rode out with one of my bitches," he said. "Bitch left and took my clothes."

I reached down for my garbage bag.

"You got to give me some shorts before the ranger come arrest me," Prospero said. "Read the sign."

A sign in the parking lot prohibited, among other infractions, nudity on the beach- "For the Safety of Park Goers," the sign maintained.

I had laughed about that sign many times. But now that I was faced with Prospero, I was developing gut-level safety concerns.

"You didn't bring any jumbies with you?" I said.

He didn't answer.

I took the trash to the bin. When I returned to my dinghy, Prospero was standing beside it, looking like the god of a sub-Saharan fertility cult. He waded into the water. I dragged the dinghy off the sand (he didn't offer to help.) He rolled in and sat on one of the float tubes, dripping and shining in the morning sun.

"Man," I said. "What's your game?"

"What, you ain't never seen no black dick before?" he said.

"Jesus, Prospero."

"Jesus ain't got nothing to do with it," he said.

I cranked the motor and drove two hundred yards to my boat. Down below I found a cigarette lighter and a pair of shorts and tossed them to Prospero in the cockpit. When I climbed out a couple of minutes later with my cup of coffee, the shorts were lying beside him on the cockpit seat. The spliff was already burning. He blew two columns of smoke from his nostrils and passed the joint to me.

This thing was... well, it was intimidating. I mean the last thing in the world you want to do is get caught looking at another guy's...

"That's a big dick, ain't it," Prospero said, laughing in clouds of smoke.

"Man, put some clothes on," I begged.

He put the shorts on, but, well, the shorts weren't long enough.

I just shook my head and looked away.

"These shorts ain't big enough, Francis Bay," Prospero said. "I'm liable to catch cold."

"What is your deal?" I said. "Who the hell are you?"

Prospero got very serious all of a sudden.

And then... It's hard to describe.

It was as if there were total eclipse of the sun.

I'm serious. It was as if all of nature had instantaneously entered a strange, surreal moment. Have you ever experienced a total solar eclipse? I've seen three in my lifetime. A solar eclipse is the closest I've ever seen to what happened at that moment on my boat.

It doesn't really get dark during a total solar eclipse. There is just the strangest, most surreal type of sunlight. Not light, but darkness visible, as Milton said about a different place entirely than Francis Bay.

Not light, but darkness visible. Those were the words that occurred to me in that instant, and I wondered deeply.

"I'm an obeah man," Prospero said. He said it like, "My name is Bond. James Bond."

"I'm sorry," I said. "I don't know what that means."

"Of course you don't."

"Obeah," he said. "You would probably call it voodoo."

"So you're some kind of voodoo priest?"

"I am the priest," he said. "I am the high priest." Prospero knocked the burning tip of the spliff overboard. It sizzled when it hit the water.

"You getting too fucked up to hear about this," he said.

He was right. I was profoundly stoned.

"Francis Bay," Prospero said to me, "Here's the truth. Anything you want, I can get it for you. Anything you want me to do, I can do it. You want to die. I can do it. You want to come back to life, I can do it."

Prospero looked me in the eyes with a calm and a truthfulness that was utterly disarming.

"You can bring me back to life?" I said.

"You believe me?" Prospero said.

I sat for a while, as the wind tousled my hair and his dreadlocks. The world had changed back to its normal, breathtaking beauty in Francis Bay. It was illuminated by mere sunlight. Nothing seemed out of the ordinary. Prospero had me locked in his gaze, and I was not afraid.

"I don't know why," I said. "But I do."

38

My friend the cancer researcher was beside himself. He had flown to St. Thomas for the weekend to talk to me.

John was one of those people who have to schedule their lives six months in advance. Now he had hopped a plane on two days' notice to see me, a failed poet/failed novelist/failed intelligence agent.

"Spud," he said, over a very nice dinner he was buying me in Cruz Bay. ("Spud" is a college nickname.) "Man, you can't do this to me. You can't do this to Joyce."

When he mentioned Joyce, I glanced around the restaurant to see if anyone who knew us was there. Joyce and I used to live on St. John.

"What's the matter with just dying, John?" I asked him. "I've had two heart attacks. Before they roll you into the cath lab, the cardiologist tells you what he is about to do might kill you. I mean, it changes the way you think."

I was lying to John. I'd had one heart attack. But for God's sake, how many times had I come close to dying on the job? Death- well, I'm very familiar with it. And I was lying only a little to John. Or maybe I wasn't lying so much...

We ate in silence for a while.

There was a coqui frog in the bushes just off the patio. Even though we were in the little town of Cruz Bay, and the restaurant was full of chattering people eating expensive food, the coqui song was all I could hear.

"What if I could get you into a clinical trial?" my friend said.

"Those trials are for people who are going to die anyway," I said. "There's a fifty-fifty chance you just get a placebo, right?"

"Not fifty-fifty," he said. "Plus, I can take care of that, Spud. It's not ethical," he was leaning over the table and talking quietly, almost whispering, "but I can make sure you get the real stuff."

"The real experimental stuff?" I asked ironically.

"This trial is way down the road. There's a good chance it could stop your cancer. Even at this stage. I think we could maybe even just give you a normal life span."

"We're already old, John," I said.

"You're sixty years old," John said. "Your life expectancy should be in your eighties."

I thought about this for a while. There was another coqui now in the bushes. Two frogs screaming.

The osso bucco was delicious. I asked the waitress for another Zacapa rum on the rocks.

"You know," I said. "My career is over."

I chuckled. Who the hell was I kidding? If he knew even a smidgeon of the truth about this...

I laughed. "Very fucking over," I said.

"But what about Joyce?" John said.

I took a long drink from the fresh Zacapa on the rocks.

"And your writing," John said. "I mean what if you wrote a best seller? What if you won some award?"

I didn't even laugh.

"John," I said, "we just spent three days together last month where you told me your career was not only disappointing, but you said, and this is a direct quote, 'I feel like

103

I've wasted my entire adult life.'"

There was silence between us. The coquis were filling the air with whatever mystery that is.

"And John," I said, "for Christ's sake. You've been doing something worthwhile. You've been on the front lines trying to cure cancer. What about me?"

The coqui song made us linger in the truth.

"Would you do it then just for the people who love you?" John said. "Just because we'd like to have you around for a while longer?"

I thought about my son. The one I no longer had. And I don't know why. Maybe I'd had too much rum. Maybe it was the stress of the past few weeks, the biopsy, the long sails. The hiding it from my wife.

Maybe it was the coquis.

I started crying, again. A little, at first. Not so anyone but John would notice.

And then I couldn't stop.

FIELD REPORT: SUBJECT MALEVOLENT- DISAPPEAR-
ANCE IN ST. JOHN, USVI.

SUMMARY:

- Subject MALEVOLENT's voluminous typescript of dis-
jointed ramblings and confessions- all consistent with previous intelligence- were found on the hard drive of a laptop
computer on MALEVOLENT's forty-foot sailboat. The boat
was unoccupied and attached to a National Park mooring in
Francis Bay.

- The boat (U.S.C.G. documentation falsified under name *Bon
Vivant*, ownership by a fictional Delaware limited partner-
ship) looked as if the occupants expected to return within a
few hours.

- The boat was boarded by agents ███████ and ███████
undercover on August 13, 2018. Fruit hanging in a net in the
galley had not gone bad. Food waste in the garbage can was
still fresh. We estimate subjects had not been gone for more
than forty-eight hours.

- MALEVOLENT appears to have been in St. John for approx-
imately six months, accompanied by confirmed GRU agent

Luisa Cooley, previously confirmed deceased in Peru.

- Disappearance of MALEVOLENT and Cooley sudden, and unexplained. Cooley's reappearance after her confirmed death unexplained. MALEVOLENT's choice of Francis Bay location on St. John unexplained except for the obvious parallel with the name used as his most common identity.

DETAIL:

1. The hard drive of a computer found on the navigation desk, a nearly-new Dell Inspiron 14, contained no files other than the narrative included as annex to this field report. The computer had been purchased online in July 2018 under MALEV-OLENT's "Francis Bay" identity using a civilian credit card issued in that name.

2. There was no browsing history on the computer. There was an entirely normal and active browsing history on all his other known devices in the months leading up to his disappearance. This history is contained in an appendix to this report and does not appear to be related to MALEVOLENT's narrative.

3. The man "Prospero" described in the narrative is widely recognized and acknowledged by other residents of St. John. His real first name may be Roderick. He appears to be an unemployed drug dealer with no steady address and no discoverable last name. Multiple residents report he is assumed to be a citizen of Dominica and an illegal alien. He has not been seen, as far as we can determine from numerous witness interviews, since the incident that triggered our investigation.

4. A woman matching the description of Luisa Cooley, previously believed to have been killed in a homicide in Lima, Peru September 21, 2017, was described by several residents and visitors of St. John in the company of MALEVOLENT in the weeks leading up to the incident. Women's clothing found on board subject's boat was found to contain Luisa Cooley's DNA.

5. Many witnesses interviewed on St. John confirmed that Roderick (a.k.a. Prospero) had been seen in the company of MALEVOLENT often in the months leading up to this report. The two men were often seen smoking marijuana in public around the island.

6. MALEVOLENT appears to have used the Francis Bay identity consistently during his months on St. John. While the timing of his first arrival on the island cannot be determined with any accuracy, witness recollections do not place the subject on the island any earlier than our last confirmed date for his presence in Crimea on December 27, 2017.

7. Four Internet access devices were found aboard the boat: two smart phones, a Kindle Fire, and the Dell laptop previously detailed. The Dell had never been used to access the Internet. Extensive forensic analysis of the other three devices can yield no evidence that the social media posts triggering our search for MALEVOLENT came from any of those devices.

8. Several passports were found on board the boat: one U.S. passport bearing the Francis Bay identity, a Swiss passport with the Francis Bay identity, a Bolivian passport with MALEVOLENT's photo and the Rafael Bahia identity, along

with Argentinian and Chilean passports for that identity, a German passport for MALEVOLENT's Uwe Herrschof identity, a French passport with MALEVOLENT's photo in the previously unused identity of Francois Baie, and an apparently genuine American passport for Luisa Cooley.

9. Cooley's supposedly genuine passport, with identical travel stamps, had been recovered by local police at the scene of her confirmed homicide in Lima last February. The passport on the boat is an exact replica.

10. Cooley's DNA was also confirmed, mixed with MALEVOLENT's DNA, on the only toothbrush found on board.

11. The boat was unlocked, with several hatches open. There was no indication whatsoever that the occupants planned anything other than a brief outing.

12. Garbage and perishable food items were removed from the boat. It was left in the same condition in which it was found by agents ██████ and ██████. Local authorities and National Park Service personnel do not appear to be aware of the disappearances. ██████ and ██████ confirmed the Park Service is not currently monitoring how long boats stay in the mooring field due to disruption caused by Hurricane Irma. This situation may change next month. Internal communications of the Park Service and St. John police are being monitored for any changes. The boat is under satellite surveillance. Any changes in status will be reported immediately. ██████ and ██████ recommend clandestine removal of the boat from the mooring field if no activity has been detected by end August.

AUG. 16, 2018

#

Miranda was following the Johnny Horn trail toward a ru-
ined Danish guard station at Leinster Bay. After the United
Kingdom abolished slavery in the early 19th century, the
Danes built this station to stop slaves from Leinster Bay and
Francis Bay escaping across the Narrows to the British Virgin
Islands.

Miranda knew none of this history. She loved the view
from the ruins. She loved collecting driftwood on the hike
around the shore of Leinster Bay. She was vaguely aware that
it might be illegal to collect driftwood from a National Park
beach, but her car was full of driftwood knobs and elbows, all
raw material for the artwork she imagined herself producing
in the future.

Her imagination was florid. Her productivity... Well, what
is productivity but imagination- at least in the beginning?

Miranda had not showered that morning. She had not
brushed her teeth. She had not dressed appropriately for the
hike, and the tiny string bikini she wore underneath a t-shirt
and running shorts was beginning to chafe her uncomfort-
ably.

Her flip flops were inadequate for the stones and cacti on
the trail. But Miranda didn't particularly care about that. She
was thinking about other things. Many other things.

Miranda was utterly, utterly unaware of her stunning beauty as she encountered the couple coming from the ruins above- an elderly, white man and a young, Latinx woman.

The man and the woman smiled, said "Good morning," and commented flippantly on the heat. Miranda beamed entrancingly in return. Miranda reacted this way- without thinking- to any smile she encountered.

She walked past the couple, both of whom evaluated her physique from behind as she continued up the hill.

Yes, they both concluded, without speaking to each other. This was a stunning beauty, and she seemed utterly unaware of that.

"You dirty old man," the younger woman said after Miranda had passed out of earshot.

"What were you looking at, then?" he replied.

An old creeper and his daughter, Miranda was thinking at that moment. But her thoughts turned quickly toward the ruins and their spectacular view across Waterlemon Cay, down the Narrows, and past Thatch Island. Her thoughts then turned toward the cute, young tourist from Massachusetts she had met the night before. Then flitted quickly to her upcoming shift at the shoreside cafe. Then to her lack of a timekeeping device, and then to the angle of the sun, and then she arrived at the ruins, where the beauty of the world that stretched before her drew her attention entirely to the sublime for quite a long time.

Almost an hour later, when she had returned to her car and tossed her collected driftwood into the floorboards, she began driving back to her apartment. She passed the older man and his young companion walking on the road toward Francis Bay.

Miranda stopped her car and asked if they would like a ride.

They would. But they were only going as far as Francis Bay. Did she know where that was? No more than a mile distant? She knew, and within five minutes she was steering into the gravel parking area there.

She had quickly introduced herself and told her story. They had introduced themselves, explaining nothing whatsoever about their relationship, and had pointed out their sailboat on a mooring in the Bay.

Would she, the woman asked- she really did not seem to be much older than Miranda herself- would Miranda like to ride with them on the dinghy to the boat? Just to see it?

"Do you know what time it is?" Miranda asked. The young woman pulled a smart phone from her fanny pack. Miranda had three hours to spare before she had to report to work. Miranda, with barely a thought to safety or appropriateness, agreed to go with them.

"I have a bathing suit you can borrow, if you want to swim," the Hispanic woman said, blushing bright red.

"I'm already wearing mine. Under my clothes," Miranda said. She giggled and blushed even redder. Miranda parked her car.

The couple pulled their dinghy toward the water, and Miranda climbed aboard.

#

As they boarded the sailboat, the Latin woman boldly held out her hand. "I'm Luisa Cooley," she said. "And this is Francis Bay. Francis is my lover."

Miranda was confused, because they were at that moment in the body of water named Francis Bay, clearly identified by the sign in the parking lot.

"Same as the name of this bay," Francis said, laughing. "And yes, since we're being entirely honest, Luisa is my lover and the daughter of one of my oldest friends, who is not aware that she and I are lovers. Neither is my wife."

There was a very awkward silence.

Miranda felt quite uncomfortable.

"Would you like to take a tour?" Luisa said, gesturing down the companionway.

Miranda hesitated, but she did want to explore the boat below decks. From what she could see through the companionway, it was beautiful, with wonderfully varnished woodwork and brightly colored fabrics.

She went below with Luisa, who quickly showed her everything. There were bedrooms and bathrooms, two of them! And a kitchen and a seating area, but it was all so compact. It looked comfortable. Miranda began to imagine herself living in this floating, elegant tiny-home.

"I'm sorry if I made you uncomfortable about the lover thing," Luisa said. "It's just we had a long discussion all morning, and we decided it's time we start being honest with ourselves and with others."

"Oh no," Miranda said.

Luisa looked shocked.

"No, I mean I wasn't judging," Miranda said.

Luisa looked as if she were going to cry.

"I'm sorry," Luisa said. "It's just I'm a little overwhelmed. This is a lot to handle."

Miranda didn't know what to do. She wanted to run away, but she couldn't. She was frozen.

"He's my father's best friend from college," Luisa said, whispering. "I know his wife. She thinks I'm her friend."

There was another awkward silence.

"I thought he was older," Miranda said. Then she wished she hadn't said that.

"He had a son my age. Our age," Luisa said in a low voice. Francis seemed to be walking around on deck near the bow of the boat. He was out of earshot. Maybe?

"The son died," Luisa said. "It's all so... so fucking complicated."

Miranda had no idea what to say. This was far too much, far too soon.

"I'm sorry," Luisa said, composing herself. "You came out here to go swimming." She pulled her shirt over her head and revealed that she, too, was wearing a bikini. "Come on," she beckoned, sliding out of her shorts. "It's the perfect thing after a hike."

Miranda slipped off her clothes and flip flops, thankful for the distraction. She followed Luisa out of the boat, onto the swim scoop, and dove into the water.

Francis was busily inspecting something on the foredeck.

"Come in," Luisa called to him.

"I'm going to work on this windlass," he said. "You two swim. You want the snorkel stuff?"

"Want to go find sea turtles?" Luisa asked Miranda.

"Sure," Miranda said.

\#

They found turtles feeding over the sea grass beds. The turtles, untroubled by the women's presence, fed peacefully as the women hovered overhead, dived, and swam with them. At times the turtles turned to look Miranda in the eye.

Miranda saw a preternatural serenity in the turtles' gaze.

Luisa was a beautiful woman. She was almost as beautiful as Miranda, although Miranda had no real notion of how beautiful she herself was. She remarked how Luisa's breasts were shaped differently in the water, as if they had become weightless.

They swam for quite some time, until Miranda stuck her head out of the water and pulled her snorkel from her mouth.

"Aren't they the most sublime creatures?" Luisa said.

Miranda didn't answer. This was not what she had planned to talk about. She thought a moment, quite intensely, and then nodded her head.

"I've got to go to work," she said.

"Oh," Luisa said. "I'm sorry. Where do you work?"

Miranda told her the name of a restaurant in Cruz Bay.

"Thank you for swimming with me," Luisa said.

"I've got to get my shorts," Miranda said. "Can you take me back to my car?"

When they returned to the boat, Francis asked if it would be inconvenient for Miranda to give him a lift. He needed to visit to the hardware store in Cruz Bay.

Miranda didn't mind. Or at least she didn't let on that she minded.

Luisa took them to the beach in the dinghy.

Miranda and Francis climbed into Miranda's car.

Miranda drove a couple of miles. They were on a narrow, one-lane section of the road to Maho Bay when Miranda screamed.

"What?" Francis said. He grabbed her arm.

Miranda braked the car to a screeching halt. She flung open her door and jumped out, leaving the car in gear.

Francis had to flip the shift lever to stop the car rolling.

Miranda saw an almost-naked black man in the back seat, smiling.

He was naked except for something that looked like a loin cloth.

"Who the hell are you?" Miranda shouted, staring at the man through the window. He smiled back at her.

Francis followed her stare into the absolutely empty back seat.

"Miranda," he said, with concern. "What do you see?"

"Who is that man?" she shouted, pointing at the empty space in the back seat.

"Jesus," Francis said.

"Get him out of there!" Miranda shouted. "Get the hell out of my car!"

And the man simply disappeared.

Miranda screamed again.

"Jesus," Francis said.

"What in God's name?" Miranda shouted. She was becoming hysterical.

"God has nothing to do with it," Francis said. "I'm afraid he's following me."

"What are you talking about?" Miranda said. "He was just there. Then he was just fucking..."

"Miranda," Francis said. "You have seen a jumbie."

#

Another car stopped behind them. The man driving it leaned out his window and asked if everything was o.k. By this time Francis and Miranda were both standing in the road. Their car doors were open.

Francis assured him everything was fine. When Miranda recoiled from Francis's touch, the tourist had grave doubts.

"Are you sure you're o.k.?" the tourist asked her.

There was a silence. Miranda had a rather blank expression.

"With him?" the tourist said, opening his door.

"No, no," Miranda slowly said. "I'm o.k. He's o.k. Really."

"You're sure?" By this time, the tourist had opened his car door and climbed out.

"I just saw a fucking ghost," Miranda said. She jumped into the driver's seat of her car.

"She did," said Francis, and he got in the passenger seat.

Miranda drove on toward Cruz Bay. The tourist in his rental car followed close behind her the entire way.

As they rode, Francis explained to Miranda just what a jumbie was, at least as far as he understood the concept. When, after ten minutes or so, they passed the Park Service sign identifying "Jumbie Beach," Francis pointed at it and chuckled.

"I didn't make it up," he said.

As they entered the town of Cruz Bay, Prospero was standing outside one of the Dominican bars.

A couple of very sleazy looking Dominican girls were hanging on either side of him. Prospero stared volcanically at Francis and Miranda as their car rolled by.

Francis did not acknowledge the stare.

#

We could talk about the Danish forts of Fredericksborg and Christiansborg in Accra, in what is now the nation of Ghana. The Danes built these in the mid- 1600's so they could trade ivory and gold with Africans, but eventually the primary mission of the forts became the slave trade.

Now, were these forts built before the Danish West Indies company began their business in St. Thomas and St. John? An interesting question.

Technically, I suppose, you could say yes. It depends on which Wikipedia articles you find to be more reliable on these subjects.

Not to digress too much, but you need this part of the tale:

I know a good bit about the St. John slave rebellion.

I could take you through some granular bit, perhaps the plague of no-see-ums and mosquitos that came after the July, 1733 hurricane. We could discuss Bressu (because that is her real name, the Akwamu name she had when she, a proud and beautiful queen of the tribe ruling Accra in its most notorious slave-trading days, was enslaved herself under the most brutal conditions in this miserable, Godforsaken corner of the universe and was eventually driven into a defiant rage by the affliction of the insects, day and night.)

Bressu's once-magnificent breasts had begun to sag. Her periods were becoming less and less frequent. She found her sexual urges mounting as she cursed the incessant plague of insects and the idiotic, filthy Dutch overseer who had at first raped her, but who no longer even wanted to couple with her.

I could tell you how she immediately captivated the noble Akwamu men when she first proposed killing these pathetic, white overlords. We could see how she unveiled her plan to establish an Akwamu colony on St. John.

We could talk of the haughty disdain in which she held both the Europeans and the other African slaves.

We could wax poetic about her devastating treachery and brutality.

We could sing like coquis of the brilliant, grand strategy she laid out to establish trade with the Europeans, to steal a fleet of ships, enslave the crews, and conquer the islands she could see stretched across the sea to the East and West.

We could chant at night, to the forest drums, of the army she would command with her brilliance, her power, her astonishing presence.

We could ululate the utter fear and the utter belief with which her followers joined her.

Think of Bressu now, after her year of rebellion and revolution, after her bold, terrifying fight against the combined forces of Europe in the Caribbean, after she had been the most compelling topic of conversation and concern throughout the Caribbean, and eventually back in Europe itself.

She is hiding in the ringing forests of St. John.

When the sun goes down, the frogs begin to wail. The jumbies begin to dance and scream in the trade winds.

Bressu and her followers will never surrender. They will never be captured. They will never be slaves again.

Do they slash their own throats on the beach at Brown's Bay?

Or do they jump to their deaths from the cliffs at Mary's Point?

Dr. Hopkins can conduct her research all over St. John and all through its cloudy history. She can comb the dusty archives of the Europeans. She can sift through the geographic information systems of the United States Park Service.

But she can't bring Bressu back to life. She can't figure out how to really spell her name. She can't even really figure out where or when she died.

But we, three hundred years down a long line of storytellers, can bring Bressu to life with our imaginations.

That is, if she hasn't been alive all along, howling in the night around Francis Bay.

Which, frankly and truly, she has.

\#

Francis and Luisa next encountered Miranda a week or so later.

Francis and Luisa had hiked the Johnny Horn trail all the way across the mountainous spine of St. John from Leinster Bay to Coral Bay. It was a grueling hike, with a precipitous climb up a lightly-traveled mountain trail and an even steeper descent down a Jeep track on the other side. They emerged in Coral Bay beside an eighteenth-century Moravian church, whose roof had been completely removed by Hurricane Irma.

Francis and Luisa saw Miranda at Skinny Legs' bar. They ordered themselves a couple of beers. The hike had been particularly hot and difficult for the old man, who was thirsty and sweaty and pale. Luisa was the first to notice their new friend sitting at the bar, hunched over a Pabst Blue Ribbon beer, wearing the same t-shirt, shorts, and flip-flops she had worn a week previous.

Miranda was not happy to see them.

"Francis told me you saw our friend," Luisa said.

"Man, what the fuck?" Miranda said.

Luisa laughed.

"I mean what the fuck?" Miranda said.

"It's St. John," Luisa said.

"It's St. John, baby," the bartender said, butting into the conversation.

"You people are crazy," Miranda said.

The bartender laughed.

Francis reached past Luisa and put his hand gently on Miranda's hand. "You're not crazy, dear," he said. "There are more things in heaven and earth than are dreamt of in your philosophy."

"Dude," the bartender said. "'D'you make that up? That's fucking great."

\#

So, after lunch and several beers each, Miranda, Luisa, and Francis were behind Skinny Legs' bar, in the far reaches of the parking gullies and derelict dinghies and maho bushes, lighting up an enormous joint.

And Prospero appeared.

Francis laughed at him. "You have a magical nose, my friend," he said.

"Who's this chick?" Prospero said. "Mmm, mmm."

Miranda was appropriately offended.

But she was not definitely offended.

"This is our new friend Miranda," said Luisa, passing the sputtering spliff to Prospero.

"Miranda," Prospero said. "Brave new world."

He turned the spliff around, put it backwards into his mouth, and began to blow the smoke into Miranda's upturned face.

She inhaled with an inebriated glaze in her eyes.

"Where you been, Miranda?" Prospero said.

"I've been here two months," she replied, defensively. "I work at..." and she gave the name of the restaurant on the other end of the island.

"Well, I ain't seen you," said Prospero.

"She saw your friend last week," Francis said.

"Which one?" Prospero said.

"That one," Francis said, nodding toward the strange man in a loincloth who had joined them, standing just outside the group.

FIELD REPORT: SUBJECT INNOCENCE- RECRUITMENT

SUMMARY:

- Twenty-four-year-old target "INNOCENCE" has been approached and identified for possible recruitment.

- INNOCENCE has been lured into compromising, illegal activity and has participated willingly, displaying no moral objection.

- Clearance sought to proceed with next stage of compromise.

DETAIL:

4. Subject indicated in debriefing that the assignment was enjoyable, exciting, and "easy." "Let me know if you want me to do it again," was subject's direct request after multiple drinks and two joints of marijuana.

5. Recommend Level 2 assignment begin as soon as practical, once approval received.

FEBRUARY 25, 1981.

#

Miranda and Prospero came from behind a rusting ship-ping container into the rutted, muddy parking area near Skinny Legs' bar/restaurant. Miranda was looking for a part-ing kiss.

Prospero just patted her on the butt, gave her a wink, and walked away.

"That was something, girl," he said. He wasn't looking at her.

The black boy in the loin cloth appeared again out of clear air. He stared into Miranda's eyes.

She followed the apparition, which didn't look like an ap-parition at all to her now, up the hill toward the ruined Mora-vian Church.

The sun was beginning to disappear over the high moun-tains to the west, and the trade wind carried the wafting scent of burgers and beer.

#

I'm sharing evidence with you.

I'm letting you see things from a number of different perspectives.

The story is quite strange. It has already veered into the realm of what we may believe is not true.

But surely you cannot deny it MIGHT be true.

In that process where you judge what is believably true and what seems unbelievable, you can, I trust, see that self-delusion is required. You, and I, and all human beings collect a mere lifetime of experience and evidence. Then we insist on organizing our perceptions based on our understanding of said evidence. When something happens that we don't expect, that we don't understand, that we can't explain, and that we've never seen before, well, what do we do with that?

We're not really capable, in most instances, of simply observing what happened and admitting the truth of that raw, unexpected experience. We have to insert our consciousness into the experience, and we begin to alter the truth.

Ultimately, we must lie to ourselves even to perceive the universe.

We have this story about a man who calls himself Francis Bay, a man who by his own admission is sick and tired of lies. A man who has, with all of his nauseatingly apparent shortcomings, recently dedicated himself to finding and telling the truth.

And now the truth has, in very short order, become so out-landish that we really don't want to believe it.

We'd rather retreat to something more predictable. Some-thing... something less supernatural, surely. Something less drug-fueled. Something more familiar and closer to home, perhaps? Something that involves less spying and deception and jumbies and obeah and disappearances?

But if I told you that story, I'd really have to lie.

To become a song
Did it ring out existence?
The cicada shell.

  - *Basho*
  translated from the Japanese by Francis Bay

Not one white dewdrop
Falls now from the bush clover's
Wind-waving, waving.

  - *Basho*
  translated by Francis Bay

There at the roadside
Was a rose. And by my horse
The thing was eaten.

  - *Basho*
  translated by Francis Bay

MARSHALL EVANS

Black thunderstorm clouds
Are eating the mountain tops.
Cool wind. Lightning cracks.

   - *Francis Bay*

To the rational
Amoeba, human beings
Cannot be proven.

   - *Francis Bay*

#

"These dudes be busting my balls all day, baby, when I need to be spending my time busting rhymes."

The plaint of the overworked, young poet.

"These people. Can you believe them?"

The plaint of the melanin-deprived, middle-aged tourist.

"It's so beautiful. I can't believe it."

The plaint of the newly espoused, confronted with a truth that veers beyond her previous experience.

"Tonight she'll finally let me do that thing she never lets me..."

The diabolical plotting of the newly espoused, imagining a fiction that veers beyond his previous experience.

"What if I throw up?"

The desperate plaint of the suddenly disoriented Spring Breaker, her inner ear revolting at the tide-induced swells in western Pillsbury Sound.

"Whoa!" the gleeful cry of her delighted friend, as she lifts her feet to avoid the future she induces from current reality.

"Watch that drink!"

The even more giggly warning of the pina-colada-swilling third friend occupying the upper-deck seat beside her.

"Hail Mary, full of grace, the Lord is with thee. Blessed art thou among women, and blessed is the fruit of thy womb Jesus. Holy Mary, mother of God, pray for us sinners now and at the hour of our death. Amen."

The barely voiced, secret prayer of the hedge fund manager imperceptibly moving his lips and counting the rosary surreptitiously on his knuckles, as he usually does on his evening commute, desperately trying to cling to hope after another day in a vile vortex of useless, destructive, incredibly remunerative work.

"   ."

The perfectly serene thoughts of St. John's only and ultimate obeah-man, convener of the spirits, doctor of the impossible, permanent in-dweller of the truth, fornicator of fornicators, smoker of smokers, intimate friend of Francis Bay.

"How can this ride always be this beautiful? Why can I not fully remember the whole beauty when I am not in this particular place and time?"

Sincere, silent, prayerful musings of one known, at this moment, as Francis Bay, but one holding, in alternative moments and alternative narratives, a wide variety of identities and knowings, a multiverse of stories and lies and truths, of love and friendship and profound betrayal and murder and might-as-well-have-been-murder and birth and parenthood and sonhood and husbandhood and loverhood and friendship and enmity and inexpressable complexity and interminable longing for the simple, for the merely ultimate truth, even now, as he rides on the top deck of the St. John ferry- a vessel bound eponymously on yet another leg of Francis Bay's own eponymous journey at this point in this time in this hypothetical or real or imagined or truthful and untruthful multiverse composed of and composing one imagined or truthful, all-encompassing, eternal and ultimate universe, which we all know and yearn for and fear.

"I love him desperately."

Luisa's thoughts.

"I love him desperately."
Miranda's identical thoughts.

\#

I don't know where I'm going. I mean I do know where I'm going. Don't we all?

I just don't know how in the world I'll get there from here. There seems to be an infinite range of possibilities, but only infinite into the future, not looking back into the past, which even an instant ago was frozen into inevitability.

But what if it wasn't frozen in the inevitable?

What, if, in fact, the past were as fluid as the future?

I mean, why does it get to be frozen, when it was so spectacularly infinite and so nearly completely out of our control only a moment ago?

What if, in fact, the whole thing, the whole universe of experience, being as out of our control as as it was all along, is just as out of our control in reverse as it is going forward?

The universe is not entirely out of our control, of course (you do see how that works, right? We are faced with a dizzying, near-infinity of choices in every moment, so we choose and act, and the very action itself changes the universe and the near-infinity of possibilities that faces us in the next moment.) So what if our actions and choices simply worked backwards, also? What if we could change the story in both directions, dancing though choices within a fluid universe, a universe that is as Caliban perceived it, an isle that is full of noises, sounds and sweet airs that give delight and hurt not.

Sometimes a thousand twangling instruments would hum about our ears then- (do they not?) And sometime voices that, if we had waked after long sleep, would make us want to sleep again: and then, in dreaming, the clouds we thought would open as they always do above Francis Bay and show riches ready to drop upon us- and, when we waked, we would cry to dream again. Such it is and such it was and such it will surely be again for me in Francis Bay, now that I have been liberated from time, from causality, from death, from inevitability.

Or perhaps I have not been liberated from those things at all. Perhaps I have been delivered into them. Having entered them, I have passed through to the other side of them. Prospero took me there with his magic. A magic I never knew existed. A magic I always dreamed existed. A magic that always, inevitably, simply and all-encompassingly was.

This is the truth. This is the whole truth. This is truth passed far beyond lies into fantasy and ultimately into a place beyond our childish, half-sighted dreams.

But perhaps I'm losing you.

Let me sleep on it. The dreams will come again. It's hard for me to tell when I'm dreaming and when I'm not. It's all starting to move at the same rhythm and with the same air of unfathomable mystery, wonder, and beauty.

Everyone is there in my dreams. They come and they go as they always have. When I see the ones I thought were lost forever, I cry to see them. I cry to embrace them. I cry to kiss their necks.

I cry to dream again.

\#

Maybe we ought to go backwards from here. We've been going more or less forward so far. Technically, in literary terms, we began *in media res*, in the middle of things, with a grisly bit of murder, and then with Francis Bay on his boat in Francis Bay, the summer after Hurricane Irma had passed.

Then we went back, sporadically and confusedly, following Bay's rambling memoir through his early years in international business, his initial recruitment as a deep cover agent, his marriage to Joyce, the life and death of his son, his affair with the Russian agent Luisa Cooley, and Luisa's death. We learned a bit more microscopically about Bay's experiences on the island of St. John after the passing of Hurricane Irma. This would be in the year 2018, to be specific. On St. John, Bay met the obeah man Prospero. Francis also met the young woman named Miranda. And Bay came to believe in jumbies, or spirits, who are haunting the forests and mountains of St. John.

No doubt, recently, you have been confused to find Luisa Cooley reentering this apparently chronological story as a living person some time after she quite clearly had been murdered by her lover, the deep cover agent who calls himself at times Francis Bay.

Yes, this is a problem.

We began *in media res*, in the middle of things. But what exactly do we mean by the middle of things? Wouldn't the middle of things be exactly where we are all the time?

Don't we all begin, exist, and end precisely and eternally in the middle of things?

Is there, really, any such time that is not actually in the middle of things?

If we are eternally in the middle of things, then any story we tell would have to begin *in media res*. Homer would have begun his Odyssey *in media res* because...

I'm beginning to reverse directions here. I'm starting to go backwards in the story. We've already seen the jumbling of time where the murdered woman is alive again and is the lover. We've already seen the jumbling where the jumbie jumps into moving cars and then jumps out of moving cars and appears to be an enslaved African from a time long ago. That time long ago is something we can only imagine. In this time we think of as now, it appears to us transformed as ruins of sugar plantations with dense, tropical forest growing through the windows and doorways. That very forest was ripped and sheared off by the worst Atlantic hurricane anyone knew or remembered in all of history- until a stronger one came a couple of years later.

Let's try going backwards, to see if it leads where I'm trying to take you. This may be an awkward and unaccustomed way to tell a story. We cannot really walk backwards. All we can do is stick one toe behind us, and with trepidation and fear, shift our weight blindly onto the unaccustomed foot, the one we think ought to be going out ahead of us.

Now, where were we?

On the ferry between St. Thomas and St. John.

#

Why were we on that ferry?

Francis, Luisa, Prospero, and Miranda, were riding back to St. John on the ferry because they had taken a safari cab to shop at St. Thomas's K Mart.

Francis and Luisa were going to K Mart to buy a coffee maker. They had run into Prospero at the ferry dock in Cruz Bay.

Prospero, in his unfathomable way, had announced that he, too, wanted to go to K Mart. Francis bought Prospero's ferry ticket and paid Prospero's two-dollar round-trip fare on the safari taxi in St. Thomas. We can't really determine why Francis did this. As with all things involving Prospero, nothing really made any sense.

And as for Miranda, the three other characters were standing in the ticket line at the ferry dock in Cruz Bay when she spotted them.

For some reason she also found herself traveling to St. Thomas that morning.

Now, what about the honeymooning couple with their mismatched dreams for the near and distant future? Do you want me to explain their presence on the top deck of the ferry going to St. John? The bride's Uncle Perry owned a spectacular villa in Peter Bay and had offered them a honeymoon there as his wedding present. They had flown to St. Thomas on Uncle

Perry's Gulfstream, and they would be greeted in Cruz Bay by his caretaker, who would whisk them in a shiny, new Land Rover along the North Shore Road to their destination for the week.

The young couple could not have afforded such a spectacular honeymoon on their own. In fact, they would never again experience such a vacation. Family strife, disease, death, divorce, heartbreak, bankruptcy, adultery, physical violence, ..., well, all of that would intervene, but that is a future and a story line far outside the scope of this narrative.

As for the buster of rhymes- his caretaker would whisk him to the poet's mansion on a mountaintop far above the less-expensive Peter Bay mansions. Our rhymer would bust no rhymes today. He would have no fun at the mansion. He had seen this house fewer than half a dozen times since he bought it. He would be overworked by his rap career, and his outrageous behavior would soon win him an invitation to visit his even more outrageous friend in the Oval Office in Washington. But...

As for the middle-aged, overly-affluent tourist who was shocked and appalled by the motley, many-colored array of characters on the ferry...

Well, who gives a damn about him?

Now, finally, what about the poor hedge fund manager riding the ferry home from his office, desperately praying the Hail Mary, counting prayers on his knuckles as he tries to survive another day of meaningless, soulless employment in the service of Mammon?

He was me.

It was a deep cover assignment, yes. But I did actually work at the hedge fund. To justify this existence, I gathered raw intelligence on international money-laundering activities as well as the comings and goings of a supposed billionaire (he wasn't really one) who owned an island between St. Thomas and St. John where he and his many powerful and famous friends had sex with under-aged girls. But...

You're wondering what the hell I'm doing riding on the same ferry at the same time with Francis Bay, who is supposed to be the fictional me.

Shit, I don't know. Maybe I want to show the real me would say the rosary in a desperate attempt to save my soul. And maybe it's too much of a stretch to think Francis Bay could do that.

But truth is stranger than fiction, I suppose.

#

Next step backward in our story: Miranda is following the jumbie uphill toward the ruined Moravian church in Coral Bay. She has just met Prospero and had sex with him in the maho bushes behind Skinny Legs' bar.

We go backwards to where Prospero gives her a dismissive pat on the butt and says, "That was something."

We can wonder why she didn't slap him. We can wonder why she had sex with him in the maho bushes, gripping the branches, her shorts and bikini bottom around her ankles. It is the most uncomfortable and unpleasant venue in which she had ever been intimate with anyone. Prospero coupled with her and passed his enormous spliff back and forth with her. Why did she smoke it so heartily, when she was having the strangest, the most disorienting reaction to it? What was in the marijuana? This was like nothing she had ever smoked.

The sex was like nothing she had ever experienced, or wanted to experience, or even imagined herself doing in her wildest dreams, and yet she longed for every thrust, every dismissive caress, every sweaty swaying of her nakedness in the midday sun, shielded from view (or perhaps not) from the dozens of patrons at the tourist bar not fifty yards away. She could hear their cutlery clinking. She could hear the music. She could hear the rattle of the conversations.

She was outside of herself. Prospero was inside of herself.

Miranda was searching through her memories of the past, wondering how in the hell she had come to this. What would her parents think? What would her friends think?

Oh, God, how could she be feeling that she was going to...

He wasn't stimulating... Unlike the clumsy boys she had directed, shoved down between her legs...

Well, o.k., you went along backwards in the story with me. Do you really want to go all the way backwards, to where Prospero made the first moves?

Let's just let them have this intimate moment. You get the picture.

\#

So, that takes us back to the redacted memorandum on the recruitment of INNOCENCE.

The document in question is too uncertain. It does nothing but hurl us into mystery. Mystery that may be too deep for us.

Back to moving backwards through the story. Our goal is to understand. To see the truth.

So, we are with Franny and Luisa behind Skinny Legs' bar in St. John. They have just run into Prospero. And the mysterious, other-worldly man in the loincloth has appeared among them.

Did I tell you how the jumbie smells?

The jumbie smells of a tropical sugar plantation from centuries past.

There is the sweat of the slaves. The sweat of the overseers. The sweat of everyone. There is the loaminess of the soil. There is the sulfur of the afternoon thunder shower. There is the sickly sweetness of the fresh-cut cane.

There is the smoke of distant fires.

There is the smell of boiling molasses.

There is the dung and the fur and the sweat of donkeys.

There is the interminable freshness and renewal of tropical trade winds.

There is the bougainvillea on the mountainside.

There are the bay trees damp from a passing shower.

There is the smell of Africa in the heart and soul of the dying slave.

There is the putrid stench of the salt pond at the head of the crystal, clear bay.

All of these smells appear when the jumbie appears. All who have seen him in this story have been too shocked and afraid to notice the smell, perhaps, but now that we are going backwards through the story, we can appreciate for the first time the olfactory overload that accompanies the visual and emotional trauma of each and every appearance.

And- we can more closely see now the terrifying and impenetrable mystery of his smile.

Of his beckoning and all-knowing eyes.

As if he wanted to share with you the truth he knows.

You have never been so terrified in your life.

Please God, you gasp to yourself. Don't let him take me where he wants me to go!

\#

Thank God Prospero is here now.

He is disarming. Always. Prospero is so familiar a figure. He is Rastalike, but he is not a Rasta man. He is attractive. He is a lout. He is likeable.

He is stoned.

He wants to get everyone stoned.

The only smell about him seems to be coconut oil and ganja.

And Prospero is afraid of nothing. He is not afraid of the jumbie's smile. He is not afraid of the other characters' reactions. He wants to copulate with Miranda, which of course all heterosexual men do whenever they encounter her.

But Prospero, we have already seen, since we are going backwards here, already knows he will immediately be copulating with this breathtakingly attractive ingenue in the maho bushes right behind him.

He knows how he will do it.

On the other hand, the elderly Francis is at this very moment titillating himself with some wild fantasy of doing exactly the same thing with Miranda. Yet Francis knows with near fatal certainty he will never do such a thing. He has some restraining impulse of decency that forces him to look away from the erect nipples popping now through Miranda's bathing suit top and flimsy tee shirt.

He is, after all, with his mistress. His old friend's daughter. He is destroying his marriage. He is destroying his career. He is with the scheming Russian spy he smothered with a pillow in that hotel room in Peru.

Oh, goodness! We've gone just a little way backwards through this story and found something that we need to address.

The Murder

Francis Bay lifted the pillow from the face of his lover. He was weeping. He sobbed.

Luisa Cooley (or the corpse formerly known as Luisa Cooley) was pale blue. Her lips were dark violet.

Bay straddled the corpse in the bed. Both were naked.

He moaned in agony. He fought to keep himself quiet.

His arms and shoulders were bleeding from Luisa's desperate clawing.

Francis's skin and blood were underneath Luisa's fingernails.

We are going backwards in this story at this point, so we won't go forward through the 30-hour operation in which Bay drained Luisa's body fluids into a hotel room bathtub, chopped her body into portable bits, packed the bits into plastic garbage bags, packed the bags into rolling luggage, then transported the luggage in a rental car to the sea at Callao. This would be a long story, and interesting, no doubt, in what it reveals about the man known as Bay, but it is going in the wrong direction. In an effort to make this chaotic, brutal reality more entertaining and comprehensible, we'll try to keep going in one direction at a time.

Before Bay ferociously and powerfully strangled his lover, he made love to her, bringing her first to orgasm and then climaxing himself in the missionary position. She was smiling at him when he picked up a pillow and began murdering her.

They were in a boutique hotel in Lima. It was close to midnight.

Previously that evening, the couple dined at a traditional Peruvian restaurant, drinking three bottles of Argentinian wine between the two of them.

The conversation was one of the most enlightening and truthful conversations of Bay's life.

Bay admitted to Luisa that he had discovered her role as a Russian intelligence agent. She admitted he was correct. They confessed the obvious to each other, that they had lived their whole lives as consummate and perpetual liars, deceiving those closest to them, not to mention themselves.

Yet they both agreed their relationship had been the most truthful and sincere of their lives.

We, as omniscient observers of this conversation, cannot know if the two professional deceivers were lying to each other as they discussed this. Perhaps both liars were actually being truthful at this point.

Both were considering how they might kill the other before the end of the evening.

Eventually, the truthful nature of their conversation led them to discuss these impending murders openly. Francis was the first to admit his plans. He began to weep like Odysseus when he said it.

The restaurant was dark, and the couple were seated in a room off the main dining area. But Francis's tears and muffled, momentary sobbing could be detected by other diners around them. This decidedly non-Latin behavior could not escape notice in the room.

Luisa took his hand across the table and squeezed it lovingly.

They said nothing for a long, long time. They looked into each other's eyes.

"This sucks," Luisa said, finally breaking the silence.

This is the true story of how the man known as Francis Bay murdered the love of his life.

#

While we're going backwards, we also should, perhaps, drop in a bit earlier on the day of Luisa's murder.

Francis and Luisa had been tourists that day.

Actually, Francis delivered a briefcase full of cash for the agency. He met a man in a black Mercedes parked on a rocky track in the lunar-looking desert north of Lima. The sunlight danced in fractals across the barrenness all around them.

There were passwords.

Luisa sat in the car.

We find nothing particularly new or important here. Francis had long been inured to this type of activity. It was almost as if he was dropping off a package at the UPS store for his employer.

As a cover for their car trip, the couple later continued driving North to Lambayeque, where they toured the ruins of Sipan, the capital of the ancient Moche civilization.

The ancient pyramids, which looked like huge sand dunes, were impressive and eerie.

Franny and Luisa found the most remarkable part of this side trip was a museum where they viewed the burial treasure of the Lord of Sipan.

The Lord of Sipan was the chief priest/ruler of the Moche people. In his ceremonial role, he wore an elaborate and beautiful costume of gold and elegant textiles. He ruled over what was the most advanced civilization in the Americas at the time, a civilization that began around the birth of Christ and lasted some three or four hundred years longer than the Roman Empire.

The Lord of Sipan presided over terrifying human sacrifice rituals. In these rituals- as well as archaeologists can tell from Moche art- enormously powerful priests tore human victims limb from limb. The blood of the dismembered victims was collected in gold, jewel-encrusted chalices.

The Lord of Sipan drank the blood to the roaring delight of his assembled subjects.

I'm going to reverse the course of our narrative here. And we'll skip forward to later that night, when Francis Bay was dismembering his lover in the bathtub of his hotel room in Lima.

Francis just couldn't get the Lord of Sipan off his mind.

It haunted him the rest of the night.

And the rest of his life.

Certainly understandable.

#

And now, by going backwards through our story, we are actually going forward in time. We are with Francis and Luisa on the island of St. John in the Caribbean, several months after her murder.

And here, apparently, the direction of our story makes no sense whatsoever, whether we go through it forward or backward.

Here we have to- ? Suspend disbelief?

O.k. Let's go with that. You disbelieve. I, as the author, will remain strictly objective. I will report the facts...

Francis Bay murdered his lover. He chopped up her body in a bathtub. He put the pieces in plastic bags, wheeled them to a rental car, weighted them with cement mix, dumped them into the deep water of the port of Callao, and now, some months later, he is with that same lover on a boat in St. John.

Make me believe that, you may say.

You want to believe.

You are not alone.

Everybody wants to believe. It's the most compelling thing in the world.

#

I think we've got to look at the Gospels here for some understanding. I'm supposed to be working backward through the Francis Bay story, and I seem to be having some difficulty with that, but bear with me a bit.

There are, you probably know, four canonical Gospels in the Bible. All of them report Jesus' brutal crucifixion and death. If they were a bit more dramatic, they would dwell longer perhaps on the more gruesome aspects. You know, like Jesus hanging from the cross by three iron nails driven into his wrists and ankles.

Modern studies with cadavers prove that human bodies can only be fixed to crosses and stay there if the nails are driven through major bones. Nails through the hands and the feet tear out. If the Romans had nailed their victims through the hands and feet, the bodies would have tumbled horrifically to the ground, the still-living victims screaming and spouting blood.

Instead, the nails must have been driven through His two wrists, crushing and anchoring in the larger bones and sinews there. Then one long nail would have been driven through His crossed ankles.

The pain and the gore would have been horrifying.

Then, when He was hoisted aloft, the suffering would have tested the very limits of human endurance.

Crucifixion victims, modern studies show, most likely died from suffocation, as their wracked limbs could not support any weight at all. The arms were quickly pulled out of joint and elongated. The body hung by tendons and ripping ligaments alone. The victim could not hold his head aloft to keep air coming in.

The spear in the side would have been an act of mercy. The bowels pierced. Shit running in His blood. More pain where pain is beyond your and my ability to imagine, but not, of course, beyond our ability to experience. At the end of our lives, which will soon arrive, we may experience similar or worse pain.

Well, I've wandered a bit off track. But if the authors of the Gospels were aiming at dramatic impact and verisimilitude, they certainly would have dwelt a bit longer on some of these details, would they not?

The author of Mark's gospel stopped his original version, apparently, with Jesus's death and the later discovery of an empty tomb. The earliest manuscripts of Mark end there. Later manuscripts of Mark include a short version of the resurrection stories.

But the other three gospels jump straight into the resurrection.

And this is where the stories really get weird. (As if they weren't really weird all along.)

During the Crucifixion scenes- about the only parts of Jesus's story where all four Gospels seem to agree, they are brimming with verisimilitude. In plainer English, they seem like they're true.

And then they head off into the la-la land of the Resurrection.

In all these stories, Jesus' closest friends and followers meet Him, sometimes travel great distances with Him, have conversations with Him, and don't realize it's Him!

Come on! I say.

You're telling me your close, dead friend, with nail wounds in his wrists and ankles, his bones crushed far beyond the point where they could ever carry a living person's weight again, his bowels ripped open by a spear, appears beside you, carries on a conversation, walks through walls and locked doors, lets you stick your fingers in his wounds, and you can't recognize it's Him?

Until, of course, you do recognize it's Him, and you tell the story, and it becomes one of the most widely accepted mass delusions in all of human history, completely changing the world, becoming eventually the religion of the very empire that tortured and killed your friend, so that people eventually are tortured and killed by the dozens and hundreds and thousands and millions if they even question this absurd and utterly unbelievable story...

Well, there.

I got that out. Surely you can go there with me.

O.k. Calm down a bit. Let's get back to the story of Francis Bay.

We were going through it backwards.

We've come back around to the appearance of the jumbie in Miranda's car between Leinster Bay and Maho Bay.

You didn't really believe that the first time you read it, did you?

#

I've told you how the jumbie smelled.

Miranda smelled him before he appeared. It was the smell of a different world that instantly materialized in exactly the place Francis and Miranda were traveling through. In Francis and Miranda's time, they were tourists in a U.S. National Park. In the jumbie's time, he was an enslaved man on a Danish sugar plantation. The location was the same.

The times were very different.

Yet here, in this moment, the times were precisely the same. The spirit was the same. The smells were the same. The sights- well, we can say they were the same, but they were all jumbled up, weren't they? Everyone was in an automobile. Just a few months before, Hurricane Irma had shorn the lush forest, slashing like a giant string-trimmer, and the foliage was only now beginning to recover.

The air conditioning of Miranda's car was running. The jumbie's smells wafted in the cool, conditioned air, along with the smell of Miranda's driftwood collection on the floorboard, and the salt smell from her swim a few minutes earlier in Francis Bay. And Francis Bay's old man smell. Old man breath. Old, white man sweat.

They were all there, jumbled together in a place they shouldn't be. In a place they couldn't be together. If you want to be physical about it- if you imagine, as Einstein did, that there are only four dimensions, then three of the dimensions at this moment were coherent- the three dimensions of place. The dimension of time had been breached.

But there are more things in heaven and earth than are dreamt of in our philosophies. How many dimensions are there really? Modern physicists say there are more than Einstein himself dreamt of.

Surely these scientists don't know any better than Francis, or Miranda, or the jumbie in the back seat.

Do they know any better than the turtles swimming ethereally in Francis Bay? Did the turtles know any better when Luisa, a creature obviously out of time at that point, was swimming with Miranda, who so apparently was in time at that point?

Luisa was dead already. She was dismembered, her body parts encased in concrete and plastic and dumped into the port of Callao. Her murder had been investigated by Peruvian federal police. Her murder and death were known and established to the intelligence agencies who would care about such a thing. Her father....

Well, her father just didn't know where she was. He loved her. But she was, to him, in that place where the people we love go- when we no longer know where they are.

We all know how that works.

There's nothing unfamiliar there.

\#

What I'm leaving out here as we go backwards through the story is the magical Negro.

"What?" you're saying.

"Do you mean the jumbie?"

No. I mean Prospero.

Spike Lee coined the term "magical Negro" to describe a stock character in American fiction. Lee identified Bagger Vance or John Coffey (the black prisoner in *The Green Mile)* as examples. The magical Negro exists solely to save the white people in the film, according to Lee. The famous director says magical Negroes don't have real personalities. They don't have real backgrounds or real families or real personal histories. The magical Negro apparently doesn't have any baggage from the centuries-long trauma of being born black in America. He just has magical powers that save white people and make them feel good about themselves. Then the white people can love a black person without having to actually get to know a real black person.

These white people go to the movies looking for redemption. There, in the movies, black people are nice. The white people love the black people. The black people love them. All must be right with the world. And the white people are not racists, by the way. They don't even say "nigger" any more. Not in public, at least.

I skipped over that little snippet of a scene where Miranda and Francis drive into Cruz Bay. They're still shaken up by the appearance of the jumbie. And there on the corner is Prospero, with two Dominican girls hanging off of him.

He glares malevolently at Francis and Miranda as they drive past.

Are the Dominican girls magical negroes to Prospero? For the purposes of this story, they have no background, no real life, no real problems that must be shared with their paying customer. They need no development. They just make the customer feel really good.

Oh, we're being distracted here. The thing we have to explore at this moment in our backwards journey is why Prospero the magical Negro is doing that unmagical thing of glaring malevolently at Francis Bay.

Let's talk a bit more about obeah. Or voodoo. Or jumbies. Or zombies.

You know these things exist, right? You've heard of them all your life. But they don't really exist, do they? They're just a bunch of fictional, magical Negroes dancing around in their magical islands by firelight doing magical, mysterious Negro stuff.

You probably wouldn't want to be there with them.

But Francis Bay had been there.

Oh Jesus, had he.

#

That wasn't in the first telling of our tale. The straightforward part. It didn't really fit in there.

We're going backwards in our tale now. We examine for the second time the agency document describing what the agents found on Francis's abandoned sailboat in Francis Bay. The discoverers tell of various passports belonging to Francis, or the man often known as Francis, identified in the field report as MALEVOLENT. He has also been identified, in a document that appears to be from the same agency many years earlier, as INNOCENCE.

Francis, the agents found, had been on board the boat but now had disappeared.

Luisa Cooley had recently been on the boat with him. They found her passport- a document that, unlike MALEVOLENT's documents, actually appeared to be real. Except...

Except these agents, who apparently thought of time as a dimension that unfolded in one inescapable direction, were mystified because Luisa had in the not-too-distant past been murdered, chopped up, and tossed into the sea by her lover, MALEVOLENT.

This mystery, it appears, will lead us into the forests of St. John. Into the darkness.

Let us go there.

What could be more natural? A magical Negro takes us by the hand, as he took MALEVOLENT, and leads us away from the beach into the forest.

The beach is on the little island at the mouth of Francis Bay. The ruined customs house there seems to have voodoo offerings posed around it. A small number of tourists have visited during the day, coming in their dinghies or paddling on their boards. It's really a long way to go on a paddle board.

No tourists go out there at night. There are sharks in the water. It's too far. There are more familiar and more welcoming places all around, and, well, you've seen the animal skulls and the strangely carved coral talismans- stuff that would make you stay away, right?

Now someone has Francis Bay by the hand, and he is leading him up from the rocky beach in the pitch darkness. There is no moon.

The magical Negro is not even real. It is the man in the loincloth.

But he feels so real. Real flesh. Real bone. Real cold. Cold as a corpse. As cold as Luisa's body once it was drained of fluids and tucked in the plastic bags.

Why had MALEVOLENT let this imaginary being lead him here? Why was he letting himself be taken into the darkness behind the beach?

You wouldn't go there, would you?

But you have never cut up your lover in a hotel room bathtub.

You've never thrown your son through a window in Warsaw.

At least I hope you haven't.

How could MALEVOLENT have become so evil?

How could INNOCENCE have become MALEVOLENT?

And how could MALEVOLENT now be walking into an obeah ceremony in the Caribbean with a non-being who was so coldly and so tangibly a real being, knowing that he was walking far out of the world he had known and far into a world that he and we would like to believe does not even exist?

Well, he went there because he had to. His continued existence depended on it. He had to go there simply because he could not imagine any other outcome. His ability to plan, to plot, to react, had been exhausted. He knew he was being hunted. He knew it was all over. He was going to be terminated. Or he was going to die the lingering, horrific death he truly deserved. There was no escape. If he tried to sail away in the middle of the night he would be followed. He was being watched, he knew.

Prospero had fed him enough ganja that afternoon to get this much out of him.

"I always knew you were a bad man," Prospero said.

"You have no idea," Francis said.

"Oh, I think I do," Prospero said. "It don't take a lot of imagination, my friend."

They were in the cockpit of Francis's boat, wet from a swim and dazed by the sunlight and the pot they had smoked.

"You want to disappear?" Prospero said.

"It would be convenient," Francis said.

"Do you believe," Prospero said, and he leaned forward to stare deeply into his friend's eyes, "that I can make you disappear?"

"Sure."

"Do you believe I can make you dead and bring you back to life?"

Francis thought about this. He thought about the jumbie who touched him in Prospero's car. This had been an experience completely outside anything he had ever imagined. Anything he had ever dreamed. A ghost, or something like a ghost, was there. It reached out and touched Francis. Then it was not there.

Francis felt a fear and an overwhelming transcendence. Yes, that was the word, a transcendence.

Francis laughed. "You're going to make me a zombie?" he said. "Or what do you call them? A jumbie?"

The jumbie appeared beside Francis on the cockpit seat. He laughed with Francis.

"Jesus!" Francis screamed, jumping aside.

"Jesus!" the jumbie screamed, leaping and shoving his face against Francis's face. His face was stone cold, as was his breath.

And then the jumbie disappeared.

"Do you believe?" Prospero said.

"Jesus," Francis said. He was gasping for breath.

"He ain't got nothing to do with it," Prospero said.

#

Now Francis Bay is holding the jumbie's very real, very dead hand in the darkness as the creature leads him into the maho bushes behind the beach. They are headed into seemingly impenetrable vegetation and darkness. The full moon lights the beach and the bay and mountains behind them as if it were day but not day.

Ahead of them is preternatural darkness. Francis cannot see.

"Come in," he hears Prospero saying to him. "Come in here with us."

But we cannot go in there with him. We can't see into this other dimensionality at this point in our story. We would have to sweep back around, bend back around in some asymptoticly quantum way that is currently beyond our abilities to bend around in time and place.

The creature known as Francis Bay, a creature with multiple identities and multiple ways of being known in multiple times and multiple places and multiple dimensionalities, went into this unfathomable darkness (not moonlight, but darkness invisible) and when he emerged he stepped forth with the woman he loved, the woman he had strangled and chopped to pieces and disposed of in the Peruvian seas.

She was dressed in shorts, a tee shirt, and sandals. Francis led her by the hand onto the moonlit, rocky beach. They got into his inflatable dinghy. He shoved it away from the beach, into the gentle waves and the trade wind blowing over the hills behind Francis Bay. He cranked the motor, and they went out to his sailboat, where they made love as if...

As if all were forgiven. As if they were in love, and they were alive. As if there were no time, and as if the past as it existed were simply the past as it existed. As if the future as it might exist had simply not happened yet. As if it could not be predicted, flowing forth, as it were, from a myriad of unimaginable events that would deliver these two souls yet again into that space they never really had successfully imagined before.

Imagine this. This is the truth. This is the truth they had always sought, the truth that had evaded them for a lifetime.

A life time.

What is a life time? Is life really defined by time?

Great literature tells us it may not be. *The Bible. The Koran. The Bhagavad Gita. The Tempest.* These books tell us, in fact, that what we think is true may be nothing but illusion.

And what we hope may be true may actually be true.

Enduring mass delusion, you may think. But it certainly is enduring.

And so, as we make this pass backward through the story of Francis Bay, we have swooped past a moment in which Francis began, perhaps, to understand the truth and began to live it.

We passed this way once before, but we didn't even notice the importance of it.

As we approach it going backward, we may be mystified by it.

Let us resume our search pattern. Backward. Backward through the story of Francis Bay.

#

It was in Grenada, after my biopsy and diagnosis, that I met the real-life Miranda.

She was exactly as I have described the fictional girl. Such beauty. Such innocence.

I met her hiking in the interior of the island. She was going one way. I was going the other. We spoke briefly.

I immediately began imagining stories about her. In my imagination, she was fifteen years old. Maybe seventeen. She seemed unaware of her beauty, of the spectacularly voluptuous body that made any man, even an old man with cancer- especially an old man who had just been diagnosed with cancer- lust for her.

This is the quick, fictional story I told myself as I hiked back toward the parking area: Miranda (who didn't have a name in my imagination at the time) was on vacation with her too-wealthy parents. Actually with a parent and a step-parent. She was tired of them. She was impressed with the beauty of the island she was visiting. She was tired of the scene on the mega yacht. She was hiking far ahead of the rest to get away from them all, wearing her flip flops and bikini top and flimsy t-shirt and impossibly short shorts...

I kept looking for the family that was following her. They never materialized, so I tried to weave other hikers into my imaginary story of the teenage girl.

But none of the hikers who passed me quite fit any story I wanted to invent at that time.

It was not an hour later, after I had reached the parking area and was walking toward a bus stop, that Miranda pulled up in her Mazda and offered me a ride.

The floorboards of the Mazda were full of driftwood.

Miranda was, I would find later, a sculptor. She wove drift-wood into the most intricate structures.

I wondered if she ever managed to sell any of her works. They were quite interesting.

They were quite artistic.

They were magical, in a way.

But they were too intricate for me. I imagine they would be too intricate for most people.

And who the hell takes a cruise to the Caribbean to buy avant-garde sculpture, anyway?

Oh well...

The truth: Miranda was twenty-seven. She had been in Grenada for six months, living as an illegal immigrant. She had arrived aboard a charter catamaran she helped deliver from St. John.

And Miranda was a very nice girl. Easy to get to know. Easy to talk to.

Very easy to screw.

And kinky with a capital K.

Which turned out to be quite an unexpected complication in my life. I had just been diagnosed with terminal cancer. I was planning to hide the diagnosis from Joyce. Now I was cheating like an amoral dog again.

I had given up cheating after I murdered Luisa.

But I was doing it in the most beautiful place I'd ever been, a boutique hotel on a black sand beach.

The jalousied windows were perpetually opened to the trade winds.

The other guests were amused, mortified, perhaps, but surely entertained by Miranda's and my moaning and laughter, by her yelps of ecstasy

Miranda! Light of my life! Fire of my loins!

At dinner, in the open air restaurant, everyone could see exactly what the truth was. We blared truth to the world as we ate and drank in the tropical evening. Coquis sang like madmen around us.

Then we entertained the other guests for another couple of hours after dinner.

Honestly, I have no idea how I was able to do it. I mean, it seemed like a long, long time since I could physically do that kind of thing. It seemed a lifetime ago.

#

"This is the most beautiful place I have ever been," said Luisa, standing in her bikini with a towel wrapped around her waist. She was on the stone walkway between the two residential buildings of the boutique hotel. The black sand beach was behind her, just beyond a glaringly pink bank of bouganvilleas. Coconut palms shaded the beach, leaning into the trade winds.

I can't describe the scene sufficiently. You will now have to imagine the most beautiful place you have ever been. Then you will have to imagine something beyond that. And that is where Luisa was standing when she said this to Francis Bay.

Of course, she had not yet been to Francis Bay- the place. She would visit Francis Bay later, after she died and was resurrected.

In the meantime, Luisa thought, she was in the most beautiful place she had ever seen. She knew (because Francis had explained it to her after she performed fellatio on him in the car) that the hotel was the former villa of a British Lord, a notorious Nazi sympathizer, and that it had been confiscated for use as a "military" headquarters by the Marxist Grenadian government.

Francis had been stationed there after the U.S. invasion of Grenada in the early 80's. He had directed the "interrogation" of a number of Grenadians and Cuban who had been detained during the invasion.

He had always remembered the place, he told her, as one of the most beautiful settings he ever knew, even though he also remembered it for those most unsavory tasks in his clandestine profession, the "safe house" activities that are safe for no one, where men and women are pushed beyond their endurance and broken, where the "truth" is extracted in ways that clearly breaks the truth into a scattering of crystalline lies...

"The TRUTH!" he had shouted, shaking the wheel of the car furiously as he drove. "THE FUCKING TRUTH! As if THAT exists!" And he laughed bitterly as Luisa wondered whether the vile taste of his semen would make her vomit.

But now she had been able to brush her teeth.

Now the beach was simply beautiful. Simply serene. Simply remote and unlikely. Simply fragrant with spices.

Francis was her lover. Her father's friend. Her father had been sailing on Francis's boat just a week before.

Now Luisa was screwing her father's friend. And she was screwing him over, in ways Francis could not yet imagine. Which gave her a sense of control and power that was spectacularly invigorating.

Francis had tried to explain this sense of power to her as he told her about interrogating Marxist captives. He obviously was wrestling with a great deal of guilt about his love for that power. The power derived from manipulating and deceiving others.

But Luisa was grinning on the inside. What the hell could he tell HER about this? She was the one screwing him. She was the one delivering him to his doom.

The TRUTH? Luisa had grinned as the car pulled into the tiny parking lot of the hotel. You have no fucking idea, she thought to herself. She opened the car door and spat.

And now, less than one hour and one more sex act later, after a swim in the turquoise water of the bay, she stood on the stone walkway and told Francis one straightforward truth, a truth I can only ask you to imagine, as incongruous and un-likely as that truth might seem.

Imagine the most beautiful place you have ever seen. Now imagine beyond that.

And imagine one straightforward truth.

That's what she told him.

She became the light of his life. The fire of his loins.

#

At this point, as we work our way backwards through our novel, I think we need to discuss three things:

1. Magic
2. Prospero
3. Trump

Well, maybe we need to discuss a couple of more things:

4. Francis Bay's death
5. Francis Bay's resurrection

That should be enough to chew on for now.

1. Let's plunge right in with **magic**. What exactly do we mean by magic? It's one of those concepts, like love, that we think we understand intuitively and completely. But when we look at it with any rational thought process, it quickly falls apart. Our understanding proves to be no understanding at all.

We might say magic is something that defies the natural laws of the universe. Think about that for just a moment. What do we mean by natural laws of the universe? If magic exists at all, then it must be part of the natural universe. Since it occurs in the universe, it is necessarily part of the universe. There is nothing real that exists outside of the universe, right?

If someone dies, we expect they cannot possibly come back to life. We assume one natural law of the universe would be that dead things stay dead. But we are relying simply on our own experience in making that assumption. If something dies and then comes back to life, well, it has come back to life. The universe has defied our preconceptions. It has presented us with something outside the bounds of our previous experience. But the universe presents us with things outside the bounds of our previous experience in every moment we live.

So how do we even have the word "magic?" Whence the concept? In practice, we use the words "magic" and "magical" to describe things that don't actually seem to us to be magical. They seem to us to be-- what? Out of the ordinary? Inspirational? Or do we in fact, as modern as we might imagine ourselves to be, simply believe, in the core of our beings, that magic surrounds us everywhere.

In Shakespeare's final masterpiece, *The Tempest*, Shakespeare conjures such a reality on the stage. The characters exist and move, live and breathe and are human, in an environment that is truly magical in every way.

Audiences accept this magic as a very premise of the action of the play.

As modern people, we don't really believe in magic do we? Or do we? Is what happens on that stage or on a movie screen actually magic? I mean the part that really grabs you. The part that makes you care. The part you end up crying about. Is that magic?

Much of our modern, scientific approach is to explain away magic. To deny it. Modern "magicians" call themselves "illusionists." They devote their careers to performing elaborately conceived "fake" magic- flawlessly executed simply to convince the audience that magic doesn't exist.

Yet the audience is sitting in the middle of a space full of human beings behaving in the most magical ways.

Is it possible the audience of the illusionist is there simply trying to convince themselves that the universe functions in a way that they can understand, while the universe actually doesn't function that way? If that is the case (I realize it might not be the case. The audience may simply be seeking the truth) but if it were the case, this illusionist might be engaging his audience in a ritual of mass self-deception, a kind of religious rite.

What if our word, our very confusing word, "magic" describes something that is fundamental to the workings of the universe? What if it doesn't describe something that functions outside the laws of nature? What if "magic" is the law of nature?

2. Prospero. This obeah-man's name, Prospero, is the same as the main character of *The Tempest*. He is a magician. Prospero was played by Shakespeare himself on stage, in that most magical dramatist's final stage role.

Prospero in this book, our story, is an Obeah man. Obeah men exist. I have known an obeah man on St. John. I have known him very, very well. They are not uncommon, in fact.

Why do I expect you to believe that?

Google it.

There. Take a little break to do that, to convince yourself that I'm talking about real stuff here, and then we'll get back to our story.

INTERMISSION- (Search the Internet.)

There, see? I told you so.

Now, surely you see obeah men exist and have existed for a long, long time, for longer than anyone really knows. And you see these men purport to have magical powers. And you see some people probably really believe they have magical powers.

And you believe there are stories of zombies, or jumbies. You have heard of zombies all your life. If you Googled a bit further on that subject, you might have come across some actual, reliable reports of zombies being held in thrall by black-magic practitioners in the Caribbean. And you may have read somewhat credible- to the modern mind, at least- theories that these practitioners create these zombies by plying victims with natural, plant-based drugs. So the victims appear to be dead, and then they live in a trance for years afterwards, held in bondage by the magician who continues to drug them.

Or... maybe... No, I'm going to bet that you pretty much are comfortable with this entire line of thought. I hoped for a minute you might be more clear-headed. But I was just being naive.

Now...

3. Trump.

\#

No. I don't want you to Google him. We all know that would just be jumping down a worm hole, leaping into a vortex of lies and fiction that far outstrips anything any reasonable person might have believed was even possible any time prior to say, 2016.

Let's admit it, a novelist who invented the story of President Donald Trump in 2012 could not reasonably have expected to get his or her book published- right? Audiences will read about vampires. They'll read about witches. They'll read about ghosts. They'll read about zombies! But readers have their limits. The reader of fiction demands at least verisimilitude. We want our most elaborate lies to be plausible.

Nothing about the Trump presidency seems plausible. It is simply true.

The man lies- fantastic, bald-faced, outrageous lies- multiple times every day. Then virtually everyone in the media repeats his lies- usually as the headline of the moment. Half the people who repeat his lies then debunk them with actual facts. The other half of the people who repeat his lies pretend they are the truth, performing the most spectacular intellectual contortions to maintain that the emperor's new suit of clothes, is, in fact, splendid!

This has become the "reality" at the center of government in the United States of America.

You know this. You know it all. I don't need to convince you of the truth. Everyone knows the truth about Trump. They just...

Well, it's kind of a magical thinking, isn't it? They just imagine what they wish were true. They ignore what they know is true. And they keep on living through each day.

Is this surprising? Is this unusual? Isn't this what human beings do?

In fact, is it not central to their very existence as human beings? They create fictions that explain the truth to make it more acceptable to them, more comfortable. More endurable, perhaps. They even begin to believe the fictions.

And they really, really, don't want to be reminded that they can't fully understand the truth that lies bare before them.

Enough said about Trump.

Or no, not enough said. We're going to have to look at the people who have died because of Donald Trump's presidency.

#

No, not those people.

I'm talking about the Russians who died in not-so-mysterious circumstances after Christopher Steele's dossier leaked, outlining Russian interference in Trump's election.

Steele himself, you will remember, went into hiding when his dossier became public, reportedly fearing for his life.

Russia today works on murder. The oligarchy, the Putin government, the Russian mob (objective "Russia experts" maintain those are essentially one and the same thing) rely on murder and intimidation to keep them in power.

The fascinating thing about the current Russian government is how it operates this way in plain sight. That doesn't seem to matter to most Russians. It doesn't seem to matter to Donald Trump.

It may not matter to you.

I don't have an explanation. It's as if the baldest, most dangerous evil were standing there right in front of you, with a sign flashing on its forehead announcing it was evil, and 1) you don't walk away, and 2) you don't really care.

You know Trump is in with the Russians in some mysterious way. You've known that for a long time. And yet...

Fortunately for a number of Americans caught up in the Trump/Russia dealings, once their names became public knowledge in America, their lives appear to have been saved.

Some of them ended up in prison, but at least they weren't being poisoned or dying in car crashes or getting shot in the back of the head on a public sidewalk.

A significant number of people in Russia weren't that lucky. This has been well documented in the public record by a number of reputable news organizations.

In all likelihood, it just sounds like spy fiction to you.

Antonin Erovinkin. Sergei Krivov. Petr Polshikov. Andrey Malanin. Alexander Kadakin. Vitaly Churkin. These names probably mean nothing to you. The men who lived by those names were real, breathing Russians- diplomats and intelligence officers who died suddenly and mysteriously after the Steele dossier was leaked.

Maybe they just died.

Or maybe they found themselves in a spot like Francis Bay.

Francis Bay had operated in the U.S. and British Virgin Islands off and on for the better part of a decade before the main action of this novel opened. He began his time in the islands working with Fortz's international finance and tax operation in Tortola. Later he worked for a hedge fund in St. Thomas. His real job during these assignments- his agency job- was to infiltrate and investigate international money-laundering activities.

In 2014, the possibility that Donald Trump would ever play an important role in the government of the United States was simply laughable. When Francis Bay began to report on the Trump Organization's rumored connections with Russian money-laundering operations, the only interest in the agency was a tittering laughter. This celebrity "billionaire," the reality TV star, might be feeding off Putin's kleptocracy. The agency didn't care about Donald Trump. They didn't take him seriously. Few people anywhere on earth took Donald Trump very seriously in 2014.

Francis Bay was in the waning years of his career- assigned to a beautiful, tropical backwater where there was little chance he could cause trouble. Through his own ever-so-slight ineptitude, through his own insistence on documenting things the agency really didn't care about, he created a cache of raw intelligence reports in the files of the U.S. intelligence community that would become very, very inconvenient in the near (if completely unforeseeable) future.

It's a story that is somewhat familiar to us: Vladimir Putin's intelligence services elevating a loser of infinitely corrupt character to a position of central importance- perhaps simply by accident.

But enough about Trump.

#

4. The death of Francis Bay. And...

5. His resurrection.

We all will be dead.

Not as many of us run a chance of being murdered by order of Vladimir Putin.

The usual fate of a Russian asset that becomes dangerous or inconvenient for Vladimir Putin is just that.

But is it fair to single out the Russians for killing people who are inconvenient? Don't people who become very inconvenient to intelligence services sometimes simply cease to exist? Quietly? Off the grid? They fall out of airplanes. They die of mysterious ailments- like bullets in the head- like automobile accidents- like nerve agents smeared on their doorknobs (or dinghy motors)- like poison umbrella tips.

And Francis Bay was as quiet and as anonymous as such a person could be. Like a child molester's runaway victim...

When Francis Bay was preparing reports for his agency superiors, raw human intelligence reports, as these things are known, he was simply passing along information about individuals and corporate entities who might be engaged in illicit or unsavory activities around the world. The Caribbean basin is a hotbed of money-laundering, much of which passes electronically through the banking system in Road Town, the capital of the British Virgin Islands.

Laundering money in the British Virgin Islands is, by design, almost as convenient and pleasant as chartering a yacht there.

Francis Bay, or the entity known at this time as Francis Bay, was merely performing the routine tasks of clandestine employment he had carried out for several decades, documenting raw, human intelligence.

How the Russians got murderously involved was a mystery to Francis Bay. He found it difficult to believe (but NOT impossible to believe) that someone at the agency might deliver him to the Russians.

But the Luisa affair had been a spectacular mess. It was the kind of mess that could lead to cold-blooded clean-up methods. Bay knew that. He knew just how quiet, deadly, and silent such clean-ups could be.

Bay's doom didn't develop overnight. It would take the unfolding of eventualities that were difficult to imagine in 2014. You couldn't have imagined them. I couldn't have imagined them. Francis and Luisa couldn't have imagined them. Vladimir Putin and Donald Trump couldn't have imagined them.

It's as if some magical, guiding hand took Francis Bay's insignificant career, tossed it in a salad bowl with his personality and petty ineptitude, and cast the whole concoction off a cliff, so it fluttered down through an infinity of eventualities.

And a few years later, for reasons that became increasing clear to Francis himself, Bay was a dead man.

He was desperately looking for a way out of that condition.

You and I may be entirely agnostic- perhaps that's not strong enough- we are probably entirely atheistic about Prospero's claim that he could make someone dead and bring them back to life. We don't believe that hokey and would pay no attention to a stoned, naked man seated in the cockpit of a sailboat in Francis Bay who claimed to be able to perform such nonsense.

However, at that particular point in time, the peculiar unfolding of infinite possibilities across the universe had rendered Francis Bay desperate to believe.

And is it just possible- now stop here a moment and think about this- is it just possible that Bay's very desperation, his frantic ability to latch on to what he thinks may be his only possible hope for deliverance, that this desperation might have opened up Francis Bay to discovering something that had eluded him all his life- that thing he had wanted so badly and never could find- is it possible that these unlikely eventualities delivered Francis Bay, in the end, to the truth?

.

#

Backward. Backward. We come now to Bay's ramblings about first meeting his wife Joyce, their early sexual relationship, and Bay's sad hints about his own relationship with his mother.

What a mess. We have to wander back and forth through Francis Bay's life, death, and resurrection if we want to understand the mess that is this man.

Perhaps we should meet the mother of the man we have come to know as Francis Bay. She really was a lovely person. Jet black hair. A stunning beauty. A wicked, flirtatious smile, eyes that always seemed to be taunting, and the kind of body that would make men think immediately of the dirty things they wanted to do with her.

Doing those things to her usually didn't prove to be much of a challenge.

Young Francis was known as young Henry in his early life- Henry Barnes, or Henry Floyd, or Henry Stevens- it all depended on which town they were living in. Henry- or let's just keep it to Francis- we've already established his names were myriad- Francis was a handsome lad, a smooth talker from an early age, quick to make friends and always quick to charm adult women. Most observers thought the boy seemed to be very attached to his mother.

There was no father around. The father was an utter fiction. But of course he couldn't have been fictional. He had to be real. It's just that he never revealed himself to Francis/Henry.

Mary- Francis's mother- floated through the universe on ethereal whims of fancy. Francis never attended the same school two years in a row. There was a string of abusive step-fathers. Mary always coupled with drunks. Beaters. Furniture breakers. She wouldn't let them beat the boy, but they beat her.

Once, when Francis was fourteen, he happened upon such a beating. Mary was naked, cowering against the cabinets in the kitchen, as the bastard- Norman was his name- was slapping her and cursing.

Francis entered the back doorway from basketball practice.

Francis was not a particularly large or strong fourteen-year-old. He was tall and lanky.

People who knew him (although no one ever knew him very well in all those towns they passed through) would say he was a peaceful boy.

Not at this moment. Francis/Henry broke Norman's nose on the first punch. He beat Norman's face beyond recognition. Then he picked up a cast iron frying pan and beat Norman unconscious, leaving his stepfather lying on the floor with a skull fracture.

Norman arose the next morning and left. He never came back.

Mary and Francis/Henry left town that week. They left no forwarding address.

This was Henry/Francis's life. He was a brilliant student. When he was a senior living in Macon, Georgia, he scored so high on the Scholastic Aptitude Test his guidance counselor suggested he apply for a scholarship to Georgia Tech. By this time in his life, the name was Francis Bay. Brilliant, young Francis dreamed of studying literature and becoming a poet.

At Georgia Tech though, he was encouraged to study aeronautical engineering. Francis Bay, a child who never really had a name, never really had any sort of concept of self, either. Perhaps a bit of self-knowledge would have enabled him to follow his true passions in life. One wonders. Instead, Francis graduated with an engineering degree and soldiered on to his first job with Fortz.

There. There's something to be said for moving backwards through a story. It begins to fill in a bit, doesn't it?

Does this any of this background help when we revisit Francis's first encounter with the woman who would become his wife? He takes his comely coworker to a bar. She drinks as hard as he does. They proceed to bed. That's nothing special. Young Francis had been doing that with women since he was seventeen years old. Mary had raised a reliable philanderer.

But there was something different about this woman, Joyce. If we go back to Francis's narrative:

Joyce told me the truth. Joyce told everyone the truth- as far as I could tell. She expected other people to tell it to her, and she knew when they didn't. She could navigate comfortably within the bounds of naked reality.

When she first told me she loved me, lying in a bed in my Amsterdam flat, she was telling the truth, the whole truth, and nothing but the truth, I now believe. But I couldn't believe her then. How could anyone love me?

I think we can let that passage speak for itself.

#

One of the possible signs of a saint, the miraculous signs that seem to disobey our fundamental understanding of the universe, is bilocation.

There are numerous, documented and carefully-researched stories of living saints being in two locations at the same time. Eyewitnesses and other corroborating evidence prove Saint A was in town B at the same time that he or she was in town C, quite some distance away.

Google it.

There are numerous, age-old stories of bilocation, across the millenia, across a wide variety of religions, even. You can look at them yourself and decide.

These stories, as outrageous- as inconvenient- as they might be, seem to keep popping up.

They might be true, or they might not.

What blocks belief of these stories is absolute faith in the reality and unity of time.

Time, most of us believe, is an inescapable dimension. It can be measured precisely. And it moves only in one direction.

Unless, of course, you delve into the cutting edge of physics, where the 2012 Nobel Prize was awarded to two scientists who proved that atoms and photons could occupy two entirely different locations at the same time.

Which, if you think about it, creates the possibility that our understanding of time is fundamentally flawed. Fundamentally inadequate. Or just wrong altogether.

Which brings us back to the possibility of something existing outside the dimensionality of time.

Think about that for a moment.

\#

Now we have some disturbing ground to cover. Bay's story of his son's suicide in Warsaw.

Why was Bay pretending he was taking his son Eric to Auschwitz?

Francis Bay had been made aware that Eric was a heroin-addict, that his son was trading homosexual favors for drugs in Berlin. Bay's employers could not tolerate such a liability. At the time, Francis was a valuable, deep-cover operative. We do not know if Bay's employers gave him some sort of ultimatum, but by his own account, Bay thought his son's addiction and sexuality had the potential to destroy his family's finances. At least that's the way Bay feverishly lays out his problem.

There appears to be no concern for the problems the young boy was facing.

Is it normal for Bay to have been concerned primarily about his job security? Shouldn't he have been concerned about his son's health?

Perhaps Bay's behavior was normal. If you've ever known a parent facing this issue, this kind of response might even be expected. We can stand back from the situation a moment and realize this reaction is pathetic. But it may simply be typical of the kind of parent/child relationship in which an addiction problem arises. Or maybe it indicates the kind of parent/

child relationship that arises from an addiction problem.

Let's give Francis a pass on this one, o.k.? He can't seem to do that for himself, which is perfectly understandable, since we now know exactly how this turned out for him.

We have Bay's wrenching regret at the words he spoke to his son. He called the kid a faggot, right there in the restaurant at the Warsaw Hilton.

And then, according to Bay's account, which seems, frankly to be about as "truthful" as an account from Bay ever gets, the young man commits suicide in the most spectacular, horrendous manner a few minutes later.

Did you find yourself wondering if Bay could have thrown the young man through that window himself?

I mean...

We've seen Bay murder someone he loved. We saw him have sex with her and then smother her in the bed. Then he dragged her body into the hotel bathtub and hacked it up, stuffing it into plastic garbage bags and roll-aboard luggage so he could transport it for disposal in the sea.

And why?

Just to prevent Bay's clandestine employers from taking action he didn't want to see them take.

We know, by Bay's own admission, that he brutally and cold-bloodedly murdered Luisa.

Now, you may ask, why would Bay admit to murdering his young lover but invent a slightly unbelievable tale to cover up the murder of his son?

Because, I'm afraid, you really can't believe everything Francis Bay says, right?

Amazing Grace

by Francis Bay

There's a place in the hymn-
Not long before the end-
Where the notes run higher
Than the voice can bend.
This is where you saw my eyes fill,
And I was chewing my lip,
Trying not to weep in church.
Standing on the kneeler you saw,
Child, (I saw it in your face)
Your father's tears at "Amazing Grace."

It came from the death of your great, great uncle
In Eastern North Carolina,
Long before you were born.
Let's go there again.
You take a right on the two-lane headed south
Out of town. The spring has turned fields two shades of green-
Light-green wheat, and deep, thick, green oats.
The sky is empty, clear,
And infinite.
The cold wind blows hard enough to sway the car.

Remember now a center pivot
Irrigation boom, spraying the wheat field
Across the road from the Methodist church.
Remember the sound of the sprinklers-
Regular, distant, sharp.
And remember the choir of the Methodist church
In their gold synthetic robes, off key,
Remember the organ music
As the church filled with Amazing Grace.
The church. The world. Everything
Filling with this hymn off key.
There's a note near the end,
As I said, to which most voices can't bend,
So high it can send
A soul to heaven.
I swear.
I was there.
His son, a physicist,
Threw himself across the back of the pew in front of him
And sobbed.

There is nothing more to report,
Than what you have seen in me, child.
And now, as we stand, I pick you up
And hold your cheek against mine,
And sing with all the others
Gently beside your ear.
I am telling you my secrets
In a prayer:

Agnus Dei, qui tolis pecata mundi,
Miserere nobis.
Agnus Dei, qui tolis pecata mundi,

Dona nobis pacem.

That poem, and the incident that inspired it, are nearly thirty years old. The child, as you suspect, is dead now.
They played "Amazing Grace" at his funeral.
I did not cry then.
I'm crying now.
I can't keep typing.

\#

Onward, backward,. Let's return to Bay and Luisa naked and drunk, deliciously so, in a seedy hotel room in Paris. Or, no. Fuck it.

At this point in the book, should I just come clean about my involvement with the intelligence community? If I really only have a few months to live, what does it matter?

The cancer is a death sentence. Long ago, I stopped caring about any oaths I ever took.

Up until now, I didn't tell the truth because I fully understood the consequences of telling. Now those consequences have effectively been nullified by the realities of life.

Sure, I had passed along raw intelligence about possible Trump money laundering. But it was just raw intelligence. I don't know if it was true or not. It's been thoroughly buried by now, I assume.

I was more worried about the extensive intelligence, some of it quite detailed, about an island owned by a pedophile just across the Pillsbury Sound from my safe house. Everybody knew what was going on out there. People knew who was coming and going.

Visitors to my house on St. John (this was in my hedge fund days) could see St. James island through any window, from any deck. From the hot tub. From the pool.

Every visitor, that is, who wasn't duct-taped to a chair in my basement.

I am more afraid of what I knew about that guy across the Sound than what I knew about his pal Trump.

My work on Epstein spelled the end of my career. It's why I no longer own a safe house on St. John. It's what landed me in a mental hospital, in the end.

I don't really think I care about that any more.

Frankly, it bores me.

That's the reality. So damn different from a spy novel. Poring over other people's mail and messages. Digging through their messy, human, usually dull lives. Spending time with all those blabbermouths. Looking for nuggets.

I stopped caring long, long before I stopped working on it all.

I kept quiet because I had been trained to keep quiet. And because I knew telling the truth might cost me my life.

That disincentive is gone now. They can't kill a dead man. And if I'm not a dead man walking at this point- well, then I'm a fucking jumbie.

#

I'm going to confess something here. As the creator of this story, I introduced Prospero the obeah man because I originally thought the story of Francis Bay would go in a different direction. The obeah man was going to offer Francis the opportunity to fake his death by consuming certain natural drugs. As you may have read in your Google intermission, obeah men and voodoo practitioners, in numerous, well-documented instances across the Caribbean, have used natural drugs to induce a death-like coma in people. These practitioners seem sometimes to have kept people in a trance-like state for an extended period, sometimes for years, to enslave them. Thus we have reliable, verifiable reports of "zombies" in Haiti, for instance.

I knew, when I started this story, that Bay was going to get in mortal trouble because of his intelligence discoveries. That was a given.

And for some reason, I knew he was going to meet an obeah man.

I had no idea, though, that the obeah man was going to turn out to be like Prospero. Prospero just came to life and started being himself as soon as I introduced him into Bay's story. I quickly lost control.

And I had no idea the jumbie- a real jumbie- not a scientifically explicable one, was going to show up in the back seat of

Prospero's car in the very first scene after the obeah man was introduced.

Well, there I was creating things with a plan, BUT- free will and some bloody other thing- is it serendipity? is it kismet? is it magic? is it entropy?- anyway, that other thing immediately started happening in the process of creation, and it didn't at all turn out the way I had initially intended.

But, why be surprised? Think about any creation story you've ever heard.

They all go wrong pretty quickly, right?

In my story, things just kept happening. You had fractals in the desert. You had Warsaw. You had Bay's son going out of the hotel window. Then you had Bay's girlfriend. Then you had him murder her. Then you had- GODDAMN IT! You had the girlfriend showing up alive and happy and on the boat in Francis Bay itself.

And there's just no good explanation how that happened. There's no reasonable way to tell how it got into the bloody story.

There we are.

Creators, it seems, ultimately unleash this process over which they seem to have no control. It gets out of hand. Things start happening that are so damned inconvenient. So damned inexplicable. So damned unbelievable.

So maybe we stop going backwards through the story here, and we just carry on. Francis Bay may be looking for the truth, but let's face it, you want me to tell a whopping good lie. That's the only reason you started reading this book, and if I don't get back to telling a delightful whopper, I'm liable to lose you.

#

Tralflamador. That's Kurt Vonnegut's imaginary planet where the inhabitants don't see time as we do. They see it as you and I would see a mountain range at a distance. From that perspective, the Tralflamadorians can choose to pick out any one part of the panorama and concentrate their attention there. They are in no way obligated to experience the mountain range as a linear event.

Of course you and I can experience time in exactly the same way. We normally experience it so. Our minds flit feverishly through the future and past. If we want some peace, we have to meditate fiercely in an effort to stay in the moment, in the now.

It's often said the only thing that exists is the now. The past is gone and the future is imaginary. But let's get real. As much difficulty as we all have with the truth, the past as we see it is usually largely imaginary, also.

Let's flit back to the past of St. John, and of Francis Bay in particular, when the supposed mass suicide on Mary's Point took place.

Of course, as we've already discussed, this might or might not be the truth. But it's been imagined so many times in recent centuries by so many people that the blood of the martyrs is said to have stained the rocks themselves red.

Jumbies dance on Whistling Cay in the night. This is the present. This is the now. Is this real? Or is this imaginary?

Can you accept both?

Can you tell the difference between either? Really?

Can you imagine the reality of Bressu, in her torn, cotton shirt. She is barefoot. The thorns and rocks of St. John have turned her feet into calloused, dusty things more closely resembling shoes than feet.

She and her band have been defeated. They will not be the rulers of St. John. They will not be the slave owners. That is their past. They imagined it into their future, but now they are imagining a different future.

And what kind of future would that be? Is it the future you imagine for yourself? For very soon, you, too, will cease to be. And what do you imagine that will be like?

Will time stop?

Will time exist?

Will you exist?

Where will you go?

Will you be dancing in the night on Whistling Cay? Do you imagine that for yourself at all? Do you think Bressu did?

When Francis Bay learned he would be killed by his ex-employers, at the mere whim of some unknown power, and- because he had lived such an elaborate lifetime of imagination and deceit- he could be erased more conveniently than he could be left alive, what did he think his future was?

Surely, at this point in time, Francis Bay would have been confronted with the ultimate truth, that he was going to die soon. This is the truth we all delude ourselves about. When you are forced to confront the Great Death, you must imagine a future, but it is a future you cannot imagine.

That unimaginable future is not far away at all. It's just as far away as Francis Bay being led into the bushes on

Whistling Cay. It's just right there. It's the next thing. You know you are going there. We all are going there.

You can't imagine into it, not in any truthful way. You can make up some bullshit. Lots of people do. But we're not bull-shitting here. We're looking for...

Why is that so terrifying?

Why don't we want to look right into it?

Why? What's eating me so?

Shall we jump off the cliffs of Mary's Point with Bressu and her co-conspirators?

Why the hell not?

#

The night is moonless. The stars are myriad.
Water laps at the cliffs' base in the lee of Mary's Point.
Waves break gently far below.
The trade wind swooshes through The Narrows just to our North.
We wonder if we will be killed by the impact.
Gravel slips a bit beneath our bare feet.
Our companions chant the familiar death song of our youth. We smell the sea. We feel their hands in ours. We feel their fear.
We feel our own fear.
And we jump.
Come along.
The rocks and waves await.
Whistling Cay lies momentarily in the clear air in front of us.
And then we are there, where we have been going all along.

#

Not light but darkness visible. This was the first impression of Bressu and her companions.

(We can imagine those places we have not been. Milton imagined hell and made it real.)

There was a blinding darkness of visibility when the jumbies came forth into being from the beings they had always been. The reef. The rocks. The crystal sea water bright with darkness.

The violent maelstrom as the sharks began to feed on their broken bodies.

They were immediately beyond time. All experience was timeless and eternal. Ephemeral and unchanging. Chaotic and static.

The sharks thrashed in wild frenzy in the broken, shallow water at the base of the cliffs, ripping at bodies, turning the water to a bright, boiling darkness. Blood appeared as it never had and always will and was so fiery, so vivid in its iron smell that smelled more like mercury. The bodies were torn, the sharks were eaten, by themselves, by the other sharks. The sharks went backward, they went forward. The bodies were whole, they were dismembered. They were whole.

There was no time and no causality, because everything simply was as it was. So, for example, the whirling maelstrom of the shark feast was the same, and at the same instant, as the whirling maelstrom of Hurricane Irma almost three hundred years later, because that time-tagging, that sequentiality, ceased to have any meaning at the instant Bressu and her brethren became.

So they were at the same time emerging from the blindingly dark water onto the shore of Whistling Cay, eternally non-corporeal now, as their corporeal beings were disappearing in the churning shark frenzy, yet perfectly corporeal as they emerged onto the beach. They held their former forms. They held their future forms. They held their eternal forms. They had no forms.

One of them was in the car at this same instant with Francis Bay and Prospero, winding along Centerline Road. And at this instant this jumbie reached for the gigantic, infinitely dark, fractal form that completely encompassed the ephemeral, fictional being that was Francis Bay at that instant.

And Francis Bay screamed and recoiled.

And hundreds of screaming jumbies danced in the roar of Hurricane Irma, shredding the leaves from all trees, dancing in the darkness visible. Singing their cacophonous songs inaudible.

This was Bressu's eternity and her ultimate reality and her ultimate unreality and her instant. No more than an instant, and no less than an eternity.

All was one, and none was one.

Nothing was, and everything is.

She was "She was."

She said, "I am that I am."

Bushes burst into flame all over Whistling Cay and Mary's Point. All the forest all around Francis Bay burst into flame at the same moment that it was ripped away in the utterly dark daylight of Hurricane Irma.

Donkeys flew braying past in the two-hundred-mile-an-hour storm, preparing to become and to cease to be in that very instant.

Sea turtles glided eternally along the floor of the bay, bashing against the rocks as gigantic waves tossed and prepared them in that instant to cease to be and to be forever.

Bressu and her brethren danced on Whistling Cay with Francis Bay and his lover, screaming the love songs of eternity and impossibility.

Luisa was dismembered and drained of blood and eaten by sharks and remembered and inseparable and corporeal and integral and hideous and beautiful and young and timeless and ravaged and decayed and dancing and screaming and singing and loving, even, yes loving with an intensity with which no mortal can love, she was loving with an intensity more intense than hate or indifference or utter disdain. She was intensity itself.

There was no time.

There was not time, for any of this. Yet there was unlimited time. There was all eternity for this. Possibility cavorted in fractals of darkness visible and songs inaudible as the complete feasibility of all possible feasibilities became completely manifest.

Prospero stroked the insides of Luisa's thighs and laughed hysterically.

Prospero was there with them, and then he was not. And he was both there with them and not there with them. He was bilocated.

He was unlocated. He was infinitely located.

You wanted TRUTH. Francis Bay wanted TRUTH.

And this- this unfathomable, incomprehensible, completely familiar experience is what he got.

And then he returned, for our purposes, to our enormous, comfortable, utterly believable lie: our STORY.

#

"It is so strange to feel the wind on my face," said Luisa, as she stepped onto the pebble beach of Whistling Cay, holding Francis Bay's hand.

"Where are we?" Bay asked.

"Francis Bay, right?" said Luisa.

"Luisa Cooley?" said Bay.

"What, darling?" she said.

"Where in the hell have we been?" he said.

"As far as I can tell, there are no real locations there," Luisa said, with a bemused look of absolute wonder, a look such as you and I have never seen a person have before. Never in our lives.

Then Prospero stepped onto the beach behind them.

"Baby, you got one hell of an ass," Prospero said.

Luisa and Francis just stared at him.

"You step in there as many times as I have," Prospero said, "you start to appreciate some nice ass. Ain't nothing wrong with a nice ass in a tight pair of shorts like that, baby. You need to go get you some of that ass, my man."

Glowering, Francis snatched Luisa's hand and led her towards his dinghy, which lay on the pebbles just above the gentle surf line. Dawn was blazing behind the mountains at the east end of the bay. The sky was bright red over Mary's Point.

"Hey, you two want to get high before you take off?" Prospero said, pulling a huge spliff from his shirt pocket.

Francis hurried on toward the dinghy.

"Hey, how the hell am I supposed to get back?" Prospero shouted after him. He lit the spliff and inhaled the smoke deeply.

"You want me to fly?" Prospero said in a cloud of smoke as if he were a dragon. He burst out laughing.

Luisa just looked confused.

Francis stopped.

Prospero took another enormous hit and held the spliff out toward them.

Francis led Luisa back to Prospero.

They smoked in some silence for a while, and then Luisa said, "Francis, where are we?"

"We're in Francis Bay," Francis said.

A pause.

"Isn't it the most beautiful place you've ever seen?" Francis said.

"Is this a place?" Luisa said. "Is this a place with your name, I mean?"

Francis smoked some more.

"I don't really know," he said. "I don't really know anything any more."

"Yeh," Prospero said. "You getting there now, brother."

"Who is he?" Luisa said.

"I'm your spiritual guide," Prospero said. He grabbed her butt cheek firmly in his hand, and Luisa didn't even react.

Just then the sun burst over the brim of the mountain to the east, and air around them erupted into song as the island birds began their day.

"Francis Bay," Prospero said. "You best go get yourself some of this ass. You wasting time on this beach, brother."

Within moments, they were in the dinghy, motoring toward the rising sun.

#

And so Francis Bay climbed back aboard his sailboat moored in the most beautiful place on Earth- the place with the same name he had at that moment- and made love to the beautiful girl he had murdered and dismembered a few weeks earlier.

And Francis Bay realized, for the first time in his life, that he clearly had a handle on the truth.

The trouble was, as the reincarnated Luisa lay trembling in his arms, and as tropic birds glided over an open hatch above them, Francis Bay came to an epiphany.

He had seen the truth.

It wasn't enough.

#

So, when Francis and Luisa encountered Miranda on the Johnny Horn Trail a few days later, they were looking for something very profound.

At this point, Francis and Luisa both did not perceive the universe in the linear way so familiar to all of us. They could see past, present, and future with the same degree of complexity...

Well, the rest of us can kind of see personalities with this complexity. The way we see a deep, tropical forest. Or moral conundrums.

When Francis and Luisa were in this dimensionality of non-time and met Miranda, she was immediately fascinating to both of them.

Her past was fascinating. Her present was fascinating, and her future was fascinating, all at once.

Miranda had been a beautiful child. She was a beautiful young woman. She was to be an even more beautiful old woman, as old as she would ever become before she transitioned into the timeless maelstrom swirling around Francis and Luisa.

Francis and Luisa were also intrigued by the parade of jumbies who followed Miranda up the trail, flying over her head and around her shoulders. The jumbies sang the most beautiful of songs. Jumbie music, vaulting and whirling as it does without time, is...

Well, it is impossible to describe its beauty.

In some ways it was as if a dozen mockingbirds were singing together in the same small bush. The word "cacophony" comes to mind, but this was far more beautiful and enchanting than a cacophony.

When Miranda spoke to Francis and Luisa, the jumbies burst into jubilant song and began to dance, pulsating with a pulse that couldn't exist because time didn't exist for them.

Not rhythm, but throbbing dance inaudible.

Both Francis and Luisa immediately wanted to have sex with Miranda. Right there on the trail.

At the same time, they did not want to have sex with her. They wanted something entirely different. They wanted to dance with the jumbies and with Miranda. They wanted to play with her as the baby she had been. They wanted to caress her as an old woman dying in a bed, moving in the final moment she would ever experience of time.

All of this could be interpreted by someone who had never experienced the truth as love.

But it was something else, really.

It was something.

It was, they were both instantaneously beginning to realize, the thing they had been searching for all their lives.

But enough of that for now. Let's talk about Donald Trump.

#

The Humbert Humbert of Presidents. Sublimely unstable. Engrossingly solipsistic. We are Lolita, touring our homeland with this predator- conspiratorial in our own destruction- while he relentlessly pleasures himself on us, as if we were blow-up dolls, and we sob ourselves to sleep at night.

If we want to look at Donald Trump from the same per- spective as Francis and Luisa, then we need to look at the timeless man, the beautiful twenty-something-year-old with four hundred million howling demons sprouting and writhing from his forehead that he had been from all eternity, if eter- nity existed in this dimension.

Actually Francis and Luisa didn't give a damn about Don- ald Trump. He only entered into their reincarnated spirit-lives because he was so corruptly tied to Russian intelligence, and because years earlier, Francis had passed on an unsubstanti- ated lead that the Trump Organization was engaged in money laundering operations with high-level Russians.

Luisa and Francis knew the Russians wanted them to cease to exist because of these absurdities.

Conveniently, Luisa had already ceased to exist. Inconve- niently, she hadn't stayed that way.

Francis was forced to kill a Russian assassin one night as they lay moored in Francis Bay.

The Russian- a spectacularly athletic brute- climbed hand-over-hand up their mooring line onto their fore deck, an amazing feat of acrobatics. He did so soundlessly, at four o'clock in the morning.

Unfortunately for him, Francis and Luisa no longer lived in the dimensionality of time and causation. So they had already foreseen his attack. Francis was waiting for him twenty feet above the deck in the darkness, squatting on the spreaders halfway up the mast. When the Russian walked underneath, Francis dropped on him, breaking the young Russian's neck and killing him instantly.

Francis sustained a compound fracture of his own femur in this fall. This hurt Francis enormously- when it first happened- but then Francis removed himself in time and causality from the injury, and he was well.

It was a miracle.

But Francis and Luisa lived in a dimensionality now where miracles didn't really exist. They were now part of the truth, and they simply were.

They needed to dispose of the Russian's body. It was inconvenient.

Francis dragged the broken man roughly along the deck and through the cockpit. He rolled him backward off the transom and into the dinghy.

Then he drove the dinghy in darkness to the deeper, swifter water off Mary's Point. There he cut long slits in the Russian's back and abdomen to allow blood to ooze out, and he rolled the body overboard.

The water began to churn with sharks.

Francis watched the brilliant spectacle in glowing darkness as Bressu had watched the sharks devour her and her companions in the same moment of timelessness.

Bressu and one of her companions sat with Francis in the dinghy and sang an African death song as the sharks fed.

The Russian himself sat in the dinghy with them and sang the Nipsy Hustle rap song- *Fuck Donald Trump*- as he watched the sharks roil the bright lime-red waters beneath them.

"Fuck Donald Trump! Yeh, yeh- fuck Donald Trump!" he sang.

"Yo, yo- fuck Donald Trump!

"Hey nigga- fuck Donald Trump...."

Donald Trump didn't exist in the timeless dimension. And then he did exist: as a young man with four hundred million demons sprouting from his forehead. Young Donald was sitting in the dinghy with them. The demons were forming a demon ladder from the top of his forehead to the top of the cliffs on Mary's Point. And thence to the North Star.

In the timeless dimension, the young Donald sang *Fuck Donald Trump* with the dead Russian assassin.

But when young Donald sang the song, it immediately took on a new meaning.

Young, beautiful Donald put his hand lovingly on Francis's shoulder, as if Donald were inviting Lindsey Graham for a round of golf.

Suddenly, round about them, there was a multitude of the heavenly host. Porn stars and fashion models-- and nymphets from the isle of Epstein-- praised young Donald and sang, *"Fuck Donald Trump! Yeh, yeh, yeh, ..."*

"Lights of my life! Fire of my loins!" shouted Donald, as he reached ecstatically for their crotches.

And Francis Bay didn't care. He wanted something else now.

So he chose to return to his boat, where Luisa was waiting.

He willed the jumbies and Donald Trump to leave them alone for now.

Boy, was that a relief.

#

The next day they met Miranda on the trail. By this time Francis and Luisa were so tired of jumbies.

Jumbies had formed a chorus line across Francis Bay and Maho Bay. They were high kicking like Rockettes night and day, splashing the water's surface as they danced across it.

The Russian assassin had taken up residence in the spreaders halfway up the mast, from whence Francis himself had jumped to murder the assassin.

The Russian was always drunk. He never stopped singing, *"Fuck Donald Trump. Yeh, yeh, fuck Donald..."*

Jumbies were having a wild party at an NBA-star's house in Peter Bay, diving and gliding from the NBA-star's infinity pool and soaring across the bay to Whistling Cay. They shrieked like children as they glided.

This activity was wearing on Francis and Luisa's patience. They wanted to have a relationship with a normal person. The only real friend they had on the island was Prospero, and he didn't qualify as a normal person.

Prospero seemed to be providing the marijuana to the jumbies at the NBA-star's house. Prospero seemed to be copulating all afternoon with a number of actual, living women up there. No doubt the women were oblivious to the jumbie orgie going on around them. The jumbies copulated with each other in another dimension all around the living women. The jumbies even copulated with the women. They copulated with Prospero.

Prospero laughed and moaned and blew clouds of smoke that Francis could see a mile away on his boat.

Luisa invited Miranda out to the boat, hoping the presence of a living woman would give some respite from the chaos of the jumbie jubilee.

And it did. Luisa found that if she focused intently on Miranda, she could begin to return to a dimension in which time was a reality, and the jumbie howls and music began to sound just like the birds and the tropical breeze.

Eventually Francis, too, began to notice the possibilities here. At first, he had simply been imagining all the different ways he could copulate with both women at once. A troupe of jumbies had joined him on deck, where they began acting out his daydreams, thrusting their loins and their swollen genitalia to the insistent, piercing rhythm of the Russian assassin's song:

"Fuck Donald Trump. Hey nigga..."

But as Francis listened through the open hatch to Luisa's and Miranda's conversation, the madness around him began to quiet. He could see sea turtles gliding silently beneath them.

There was something worthwhile here, he suspected. This young woman represented a brave new world, perhaps.

Was there another world of possibilities he had not yet experienced- even though he had experienced a liberation and transport into a universe far more complete than the one he had experienced before?

Francis found himself wondering. How could this beautiful young woman sit so peacefully in the midst of the timeless madness that surrounded her?

As Luisa and Miranda swam with sea turtles, Francis stayed on board the boat and contemplated all this. He sang with the assassin. It helped him focus:

"Fuck Donald Trump. Fuck Donald Trump. Yeh nigga..."

In the timeless dimension, Francis liked to jump in and out of the window with his son in Warsaw. He liked the way the glass shattered and fell as fractals, and the way the fractals re-combined into the transparent whole as his son passed into and back out of death.

He and his son laughed endlessly at this game in the time-less dimension.

In time, on the deck of his sailboat in Francis Bay, Francis pondered all this with a clarity and wonder he never imagined possible.

#

"Our Father, which art in heaven, hallowed be thy name," Francis Bay prayed.

He was curled like a fetus on his berth. The Russian assassin sang the incessant, inescapable rap song in the rigging above him. The bay was full of jumbies doing a wild dance to the indescribably random beat of drums in a timeless dimension.

What in the bloody hell does that mean? Francis thought to himself. He prayed it, actually, since he was engaged in an earnest attempt to communicate with some entity outside his immediate universe of experience.

"Our Father?" What does that mean? It doesn't make any sense, if you think about it at all. God is a father? A father like me? Well, o.k. We could say an obtuse, evil and ultimately shitty father, who may genuinely love his son with all his being, but who nevertheless causes his son's own brutal and needless death.

"Which art in heaven?" Where is heaven? Why does this need to be mentioned? Is it because "the Father" is off in some imaginary place, not here in reality? He's off somewhere we want to go, but we can't just go there if we want?

Hell, I'm off in some imaginary place right now, but it's not imaginary. It's reality. It's that fucking TRUTH I've been looking for all my damned life, and now I just wish I could get the hell away from it. Where the hell is this heaven? How do I know it's not going to be just as unbearably fucked up as Francis Bay is right here and now? Here and now, that is, in a universe where neither "here" nor "now" exist.

"Hallowed be thy name? WHAT THE FUCK DOES THAT MEAN?

I mean I just want to give up. It's impossible. Hallowed be thy name? Hallows? Aren't hallows like souls or ghosts or something? I mean here I am in the universe of eternal and timeless spirits, and these people, or these jumbies are driving me out of my mind! Hallowed be God's name? Oh for Christ's sake! It's just a bunch of meaningless gobbledy-gook like that fucking assassin's stupid song.

"I LOVE DONALD TRUMP!" Francis shouted aloud through the hatch above his head. "HE IS A CREATURE OF INFINITE BEAUTY!"

The assassin laughed and pirouetted around the mast, singing even more loudly.

"Thy kingdom come. Thy will be done. On earth as it is in heaven?"

MORE INCOMPREHENSIBLE WORDS! It's doing nothing for me. Francis thought, which meant he was praying, with an honesty and fervor that had hitherto escaped him during his time in the timed dimension, as well as his non-time in the timeless dimension. Francis thought of *One Day in the Life of Ivan Denisovich*, the Russian novella, which he had read as a young man. At the end of the book, after an apparently meaningless day laying concrete block in the Siberian gulag, Ivan hears a prisoner on a nearby bunk repeat the Lord's prayer, and Ivan has an epiphany of sorts. Not a cheesy, sentimental epiphany, but the clear-eyed epiphany that might be had by a prisoner stuffed away to die for non-crime in Stalin's Russia. A non-person in a non-place, where time had essentially stopped.

And to Ivan, the prayer made sense.

And so, as Francis was trying desperately trying to still his mind in this timeless place where he was literally a non-person, driven to despair by the incessant rapping of the Russian above him, Francis had decided to try the prayer. Maybe it would lead to a way out. Maybe it would help.

But it wasn't doing any fucking GOOD!

Because it didn't make any fucking SENSE!

"Give us this day our daily bread."

O.k. That part made sense. It made a lot of sense. One could base an entire philosophy of life on this phrase. "Give us this day our daily bread."

"Forgive us our trespasses as we forgive those who trespass against us."

O.k. That makes plenty of sense. I can see how that would work.

"And lead us not into temptation, but deliver us from evil." Well, damnit, back to the fucking nonsense. Why would this heavenly father, whoever the fuck that is, lead us into temptation and evil anyway? And why would praying this stupid prayer keep him from doing it to us again?

Evil- that would be like Francis Bay, right? Have I not been essentially pure evil during my entire existence? And how many people were delivered unto me? Guess they just didn't pray enough to be saved from it.

Well, o.k. I see that.

At any rate, I'm pretty sure I'm right smack dab in the middle of evil at this particular moment, although there isn't one particular moment here. This is basically eternity. Eternity in a micro-moment. Time has ceased to exist, but it seems to have done so by expanding into eternity itself.

Thus Francis Bay prayed in Francis Bay. The eternal praying to the Eternal. In eternity. With the eternal prayer.

And strangely, something began to happen.

Francis Bay was being truthful as he prayed.

#

Francis Bay spent more and more time in Francis Bay jumping in and out of the window of the Warsaw Hilton with his son.

Sometimes he pushed his son out.

Sometimes the boy jumped.

With time, (oh, that meaningless word!) Francis could not recall whether he killed his son or his son killed himself.

Sometimes Francis threw the chair through the window, as he was pretty sure had happened when time was real.

Always, Francis noticed and remarked the way his son grasped the arms of the chair before this happened, so that his fingerprints would be there along with the father's. Francis had spent a lifetime (which, by the way, being contingent as it was on time, was rapidly fading into irrelevance for Francis), anyway, he had spent a lifetime noticing and scheming, and this particularly poignant little detail stuck with him even in eternity.

Eventually, Francis died with his son every time they went out the window. Sometimes the boy even threw the dour father out the window to his death, but every time, both the father and the son died as they hit the ground in a shower of delightfully glittering fractals of glass.

Each time (sic) they died, they rose again and went backwards in time (sic) into the window, which was reconstituted immediately into a transparent whole.

The father himself began to transform in this endlessly and joyfully repeated story.

He transformed, in some way, in some way that didn't really transform him, from the terrifying, murderous, unfair father into the loving father who died with his own son and rose with him in this endlessly repeating cycle of love and forgiveness, a cycle in which the horror of the reality became something entirely different. It became an endlessly repeating cycle of love and forgiveness.

Francis hugged his son and caressed him as they fell to their deaths in the glittering brilliance, hurtling through bitterly cold air transcendent with love and forgiveness and endless possibility.

And Eric, the terrified and broken boy, so brutalized by his father's life of impenetrable lies and mystery, his father's utter failure to be a father, began to love the moments they spent together before their deaths.

As the window broke, and they went through it, the universe was a timeless place of infinite beauty and possibility. The terrified boy began to long for this very moment of passing- passing into a kingdom of heaven, really, where his father's loving embrace was always there, where the terror of the imminent death ceased altogether to be a terror and became an overwhelming hope of eternal liberation and...

Francis Bay spent more and more of his time in Francis Bay, where there was simply no time, running through this story again and again, varying it, playing with it, rejoicing in it, living it.

This is the truth.

But Francis Bay no longer cared about the truth. He only cared about his story, you see.

#

Francis Bay began to live another story over and over in his timeless existence.

In this story, he made love to Luisa Cooley, then he strangled her. That is- if he could strangle her before she killed him, which sometimes happened in this story, making it another story altogether. Then he cut her up in the bathtub, then he put her in plastic bags, then he threw her into the ocean. Then....

Only it wasn't really then, since there was no time. I mean a Tralflamadorian sort of "then," in which these events were laid out like a mountain range on the horizon, although, of course, it is an illusion to view a mountain range as a two-dimensional line on the horizon. In fact, mountain ranges exist in three dimensions. If you get close, the mountains rise amongst each other, with valleys and canyons and saddles and cols and high mountain passes and peaks you can't see...

Anyhow, Luisa and Francis emerged from the bushes in Whistling Cay, set forth upon the timeless sea in Francis Bay, and converged in the forward berth of Francis's sailboat, where they began making love again.

This cycle of lovemaking, death, dismemberment, immersion, rebirth, and renewed lovemaking delighted them on some profound, timeless level, sort of like the myth of Isis and Osiris, or maybe the myth of Persephone, or many other myths...

They found they enjoyed the endlessly varying and unvarying cycle of sexuality, murder, dismemberment, immersion and rebirth so much that they started adding an even more bizarre element. When they cut their lover up in the bathtub (when the Russian agent, Luisa, managed to kill Francis Bay before he killed her, she would inevitably hack him to pieces in the same hotel bathtub and throw him into the same spot in the Pacific Ocean)- anyhow, when they cut up their dead lover, they began eating a bit of his or her body and drinking a bit of his or her blood.

They thought this strange. They couldn't exactly tell why they did this, and why they enjoyed it so much.

Then they remembered their timed existence, just before they entered this delightfully endless cycle of death and rebirth, when they had visited the Royal Tombs of Sipan Museum in Lambayeque, Peru, where they viewed the magnificent mummy and burial attire of the Lord of Sipan, that prehistoric king who led a spectacular ritual.

In the Lord of Sipan's ritual, captives, or sacrificial victims (were they really captives- or were they willing sacrificial victims who did all this just because it felt so delightfully good that they would get up early on a Sunday morning, put on unusually nice clothes, and drive halfway across the island of St. John to Our Lady of Mount Carmel Catholic Church to participate in ritual cannibalism...?)

Anyway, the Lord of Sipan presided over a ritual in which the sacrificial victims were torn literally limb from limb in front of an elegantly costumed coterie of high priests and altar attendants, the blood of the victim was gathered in a bejeweled golden goblet and presented to the LORD himself, who then, to the delight and deliverance of the watching multitudes, drank the blood with universe-renewing gusto.

Then, after they had seen the exhibit about this ancient Peruvian ritual, Francis and Luisa had driven back to their hotel in Lima, gone to their room, taken their clothes off, and...

Well, you know what happens next.

You've seen it again and again.

Since before the beginning of time, even.

This is what they were up to in Francis Bay for some time (sic) before they ran into Miranda.

#

I am drawn again to Miranda's young breasts, swaying gently as she walked up the trail in a bikini top and t-shirt. I'm reminded of the flip-flops flopping on her beautiful feet.

I remarked to myself what a long way she had walked in those flimsy flip flops over so many miles of stones, through so many cacti.

I thought of my aged feet and ankles, which reminded me rather poignantly of the one-way dimensionality of that taut string vibrating through the universe which seemed to define my life.

I had my book. With my book I could catch this moment of beauty, and I could relive it. I could learn about Miranda. I could fall in love with her. I could make love to her.

Oh light...! Oh fire...!

My feet and ankles would not hurt as I typed.

Later that morning, as I was riding into Cruz Bay with Prospero, smoking an enormous spliff with him, I told him about the beautiful young woman I had met on the Johnny Horn trail.

"Did you fuck her?" he asked me with a devilish smile.

"Prospero," I said. I didn't say anything else.

"Why you ain't fuck her?" he said.

"Because I'm too old," I said. I coughed. His weed was so strong.

"Hey, you still got a dick, ain't you?"

"Yeh," I said, "I suppose you'd already be doing her right now if you'd met her."

"I'm an obeah man," Prospero chuckled. "Why you think I became an obeah man? So I can talk to the spirits?"

"You tell me," I said. We were speeding along the North Shore road in Prospero's wreck of a car. I was already hallucinating on his pot, with an edge that made this beautiful drive through the Virgin Islands National Park seem like a drive through the core of the universe, an indescribable delight of color and shade and light and fragrance.

There were three jumbies riding in the back seat, as I remember. I had become used to jumbies being real whenever I was with Prospero.

"Hey, you imagining your book now?" Prospero said.

"I'm always imagining that book, dude."

"You can have me fuck that hot white chick in the book," Prospero said. "You need to give me a really big dick." He guffawed.

Whenever Prospero laughed, jumbies would laugh, too, hysterically. I had gotten used to this. It sounded like trade wind gusts whipping through the forest.

"Nobody wants to read a book about your dick, Prospero," I said. "They want to read a book about spies and intrigue and murder."

"Oh, you wrong," Prospero said. The car slid through a hairpin curve, and I thought we were going to be launched into the sky above Francis Bay.

"People want to read a book about the ultimate mystery of the universe," Prospero said. "You write them a book about that mystery of the universe, the one I be exploring night and day, and you got something."

I pondered this. We did not sail through the air across Francis Bay.

The jumbies began singing in the back seat. They were always singing. It sounded like tree frogs and tropic birds and a thousand twangling instruments humming about mine ears.

"You write them a book about a magical Negro," Prospero said. "That will be a book people want to read."

"You don't even know what a magical Negro is," I said.

"Sure I do," Prospero said. "It's a term Spike Lee invented to describe Negros like me- the Negroes white people dream up- like you dreaming me up.

"Not the real me," he said. "The Prospero you imagine. The magical one who don't live in no real house wrecked by hurricane Irma, who don't have no real family and friends. Who ain't been poor his whole life just because he was born black in Dominica. Who ain't got no real family back home he's trying to help 'cause they house got wrecked, too, in the fucking hurricane. Who ain't hiding all the time from Donald Trump's ICE. Who ain't furious at all you white fuckers in your yachts and mansions and on your vacations down here in our land where you keep us stomped down and poor..."

The jumbies in the back seat squealed with delight.

Well, like so many things Prospero said, that made so damn much sense it just shut me up for a while.

#

When we got into town, Prospero had some insidious thing he was planning to do, so I was on my own. I was terribly buzzed, and I decided I needed a good noon beer. Or three. Plus I needed a cheeseburger in paradise. And fries.

When I walked into the beachside bar, who was working behind the bar but the mellifluous, delectable Miranda?

I was hallucinating still. She looked so much better and so much younger than she did that morning when I met her on the trail. With a body like Brigitte Bardot.

Brigitte Bardot! That tells how terribly far along the taut string of one-dimensional time I had advanced.

"Oh, hey!" Miranda said when I took a seat at the bar. She had the biggest, sweetest smile.

"Yeh, whoa," I said, trying not to look so high and so old.

"How was your hike?" she asked.

We had met on a real hike on the real trail above Leinster Bay earlier that morning.

"Yeh, great. So you work here?" I blubbered.

And then the three jumbies from Prospero's back seat showed up. They were standing on the other side of the bar, laughing at me.

I blathered through a conversation- ordering beer and the food of paradise.

The jumbies started dancing. I was getting to be so damn tired of these jumbies.

"Hey," Miranda whispered to me, leaning in very close to me as she handed me a beer. "You don't know where I could get some good weed, do you?"

I giggled.

"Whew," she said, waving her hand in front of her nose. Apparently I reeked from my ride with Prospero.

The jumbies were dancing on stilts now. They were playing mocko-jumbies, stilt dancers in the carnival parade. Real jumbies don't look like mocko-jumbies, unless, as in this instance, they want to. The jumbies all waved their hands in front of their noses and mocked Miranda.

I grew better at conversation as I worked through the cheeseburger and three beers. My buzz mellowed. Miranda was busy with lunch service. The long pauses in our conversation gave me time to compose myself as a man my age should, or at least as I imagined I should compose myself. This was St. John, after all. And I'd been here too long.

I blurted out I was a writer. That would give me some cred. And, shit, it really wasn't a lie.

"Is that how you can afford to live on a sailboat?" she asked.

I laughed. I couldn't help it. As if anyone needed any kind of livelihood to live on a sailboat.

"You want to go sailing?" I asked.

She thought about it for a couple of minutes while she made some drink orders. When she shook the drink mixer, a light shone into my life! Fire roared in my loins.

It was a magical dance of unbridled beauty.

"Sure, I love sailing," she said. She shook the mixer again. Jesus.

#

So I went back to my boat in Francis Bay and tried writing.

There's this thing about writing novels that you're probably not aware of- since you consume the finished product in a very linear fashion.

I was not aware of it myself until I sat down and tried turning my life into a novel.

You see, writers don't have to actually write things in a linear fashion. As they're working on the story- a new thought or story line occurs and starts to grow- and they can go back and start building that new plot or story line or character in from the beginning of the book.

I suppose if they're successful, the reader ends up thinking the writer wove together this miraculously revealing tale, where all the pieces fit together seamlessly. The reader was led to the inevitable, fulfilling conclusion all the way from the beginning of the book. In reality, the writer was just...

So... based on Prospero's ideas from earlier that morning, and on my meeting with Miranda on the Johnny Horn trail, I went back and added the character of Miranda to this novel.

Of course, I didn't call her by her real name.

I used the ingenue from Shakespeare's *The Tempest*. *The Tempest* is set on a magical island, and my novel, well...

I created my fictional affair with her in Grenada. Yes, I put her in Grenada, and I made passionate love to her in the boutique hotel, instead of telling the truth about the hellish week I spent in that hotel with a catheter up my limp, bruised penis, wearing an adult diaper- impossibly high on pain killers- while the cauterized wounds in my bladder healed from the biopsy.

As you may be figuring out, Prospero- another real character from St. John- isn't really called Prospero. His name is something else. You can't just go around writing novels with real people in them, can you?

At the suggestion of the real Prospero, I gave the fictional character an enormous penis. You've seen it a number of times. And you've seen Prospero screwing Miranda in the bushes out behind Skinny Legs' bar.

Which is pretty perverted, since Prospero the magician/ writer is the father of Miranda in Shakespeare's *The Tempest*.

As you have now seen, this magical and bizarre sexual en- counter was added into the plot of the magical and bizarre novel I was already typing on my real sailboat in that real, very magical place called Francis Bay.

Francis Bay- that bastard. Surely you've grown to hate him as much as I. The perverted fiction of my life.

If it gives you any solace at all- and I assure you it gives me practically none- I didn't really cut up my lover in a bathtub in Peru.

Here's what really happened.

#

The fourteen-year-old girl had been delivered to me. I met her at the ferry dock in Red Hook. She was towing two large roll-aboard suitcases behind her. I knew she had been one of Epstein's girls. I knew she was important. She was important enough that I was being thrown out of my own home so it could be a "safe house" for a few days.

She was preternaturally beautiful, old-looking for her age, yet she was so-- fragile.

She was me.

She was such a victim of a sexual predator.

Oh, you know my relationship with that whole subject. But come on! I never actually screwed kids. I might screw my best friend's kid, but she was twenty-seven when we started. She was as guilty a conspirator in that calamity as I. Oh fuck that!

This kid- sure, I'll call her Luisa, but that's probably just confusing you. Luisa was the name the kid really gave me. I called my best friend's kid Luisa in this book because of that.

Anyway, I rode on the top deck of the St. John ferry with the real Luisa. She was terrified. She was as terrified as I had been my whole life. I lied to her with my usual, mellifluous, enchanting lies. The lies I carried on forever. The lies I can't stop telling. The lies I can't stop telling myself.

Those lies made her feel a little better. She looked like she was starting to believe she was really going to escape. She was going to be safe at last. She was going to a safe house, for God's sake.

I drove her in my SUV to my house. To Joyce's house. To what had been Eric's house, too.

I delivered her to the special operatives. I didn't even know these guys. They had shown up earlier that morning, as soon as I had gotten my orders. But they had the look. They looked like angels of death.

And then I flew to the States for three days.

When I got back, the house had that smell to it. That safe house smell. That spiritual ambiance that made me kind of sick with dread when I came back to it, knowing the agency had used it in my absence.

But this time, there was something far, far worse.

I had a feeling of unforgivable sin.

I felt like there was nothing I could ever do to redeem myself. There was no grace that would ever be strong enough. Forgiveness and grace were just a fantasy. There in my magnificent home hanging over the Caribbean, my doom had been sealed for all eternity.

Joyce was traveling overseas for Fortz somewhere. I was alone in our home. I couldn't really sleep that night.

At four in the morning, the magical hour for those of us in my profession, that hour when time itself renders our victims most helpless, I went downstairs to the basement and began to look for clues. What madness! Why would I even want to know? And why would these guys even leave clues? They were consummate professionals.

I tore the basement apart all that morning. I found nothing that would have led me toward the truth.

So I told myself a story. I started to imagine that Luisa had, in fact escaped. Maybe she was back with her family. Oh, that direction of the story quickly terrified me, bringing forth memories of my own childhood.

No, she had been delivered to a foster family. She was with those people you know exist. You've imagined them. Surely you met them at sometime or another. They love each other. They love their children. They treat them as people should treat each other.

For a week, I concocted the most elaborate story of how Luisa had escaped Jeffrey Epstein and whatever powerful men had been fucking her, and how the government had now delivered her to live with just the kind of family I always wanted to live with. The family I wanted to create with Joyce, for God's sake. The family Joyce could have created if she hadn't married me.

And I had helped Luisa, in my stupid fucking story. I had carried her across on the ferry to the safe house.

Joyce was coming home the next weekend. I was living my stupid fucking story so persistently in my mind and imagination I could hardly get any work done that week. But that didn't matter. The agency had already gotten their service out of me for the month, I told myself.

But Joyce was coming home. I needed to clean the house. I started with the bathrooms.

I don't know why I started with the bathroom that had been Eric's. We never used that one any more, but I figured, I suppose, that the operatives may have used it during their stay, and knowing how Joyce's standards of cleanliness were, like her concept of the truth, something nearly beyond my imagination, I decided to check it.

These guys weren't such consummate professionals after all, I quickly learned. I found swaths of blood. Sloppily wiped.

Dust from the concrete pre-mix.

Nicks on the porcelain of the bathtub from the saws.

I scrubbed and scrubbed Eric's bathroom. I scrubbed until my fingers bled.

#

Boy, writing this "novel" is giving me a fit.

Now the real life Miranda (not her name) is coming out to my real boat the day after tomorrow. The boat is real. It's forty feet long. But it's not nearly as nice as Francis Bay's boat.

The money I got from selling the safe house after I left the agency- most of that money disappeared quite some time ago. I am a lot of things, and I've been a lot of things. A good busi-nessman is not one of them.

Plus, let's get real. My wife has a steady job. She makes a significant contribution to this lifestyle, even if she never spends time with me anymore.

I keep telling her if she'd quit her job she could just come hang out with me on the boat. Which she could. We do have enough to fund that simple, clean lifestyle, but that's another story...

Joyce is finished with me in reality.

For Christ's sake, who am I kidding? The universe is just about finished with me.

I was feeling pretty damn guilty about Miranda when I got back to the boat that night and started sobering up. So I called Joyce. I told her how the book was coming...

"Franny," she said, "you aren't writing one of those books that jumps all around in time, are you? I'm telling you, people just can't follow those things. You need to make the story

something people can follow."
     Well, damn it. She is the best critic.

#

Let's go ahead now. Let's go into the future.

We've all watched people die of cancer.

Now I'm reasonably sure that's how my life is going to end.

The creeping, aching pain, the pain that feels like a knife being driven into different parts of my torso, has already started.

Imagine what it will be like in a few weeks? Will it be a few months?

Will I be able to stay on the boat in St. John?

When I lose control of my bowels- when I begin to cry out at night, to scream like a jumbie, can I stay on a mooring in Francis Bay? Or will someone eventually complain to the park rangers? Will they come and find me, writhing in my own filth? Will they call my wife and cause me to be evacuated?

Will she let me come home?

Will she make me go into hospice?

Will Eric come? Oh God.

Oh God.

I won't be going to New York. Sloan Kettering will not have a miracle cure. My friend the researcher was just inventing a fiction to avoid the certainty that he has lived with every day for the past thirty-five years. In reality, he prescribed pain medication I administer myself- whenever I want. I pick the dope up at the pharmacy in St. John each week.

The real person he cared about as a friend is going to die in the most prolonged, hellish way. And John- renowned cancer specialist that he is- not going to be able to do anything about it. He's tried his entire adult lifetime to put a stop to this hideous inevitability, but nothing stops it. It remains inevitable.

It remains the ultimate truth.

\#

Now, as I face the ultimate reality, I'm facing it with the unalterable certainty of failure, little-to-no real accomplishment, and precious little money to leave the woman I love.

I was a failure as a father. God, what a failure!

Certainly a failure as a husband. I didn't really have that affair with Miranda in Grenada, by the way. I just imagined it in vivid, kinky detail, typing and polishing and revising it over and over. But the young woman I've called Luisa in my story...

Is that any kind of accomplishment?

Hell, I never actually killed anybody, either. At least not with my own hands.

I don't think that matters. In reality- in my head- I was just as evil as Francis Bay. It doesn't matter, really, how we imagine ourselves. I'm beginning to realize that we may all be as evil as Francis Bay. We invent stories about ourselves to deny the reality. But in the end, we are faced with the lies we've been telling.

Over, and over, and over. Decade after decade.

Now I will be tortured to death.

Soon.

Is it because I deserve it?

Or is that just the way it is?

Very, very confusing time. Difficult to manage one's emotions.

Thus I get high with Prospero. I hang out with him and his jumbies.

And I make up a long story about Francis Bay. One that is too complex.

Why don't I write some nice poems about God or something?

I guess you might say I'm over that shit.

So over it.

I'm into jumbies now, and I'm trying to figure that out.

#

How did I first come to see jumbies? Real jumbies?

It wasn't the way I've imagined Francis Bay beginning to see them. I didn't think you'd believe the way I saw them.

In reality, they began to hang around the periphery of the conversation when I smoked pot with Prospero.

They were there, but I didn't notice them.

At first, I thought they were just other people.

I didn't talk to them, and it didn't really register that they were dressed in a loincloth or in eighteenth-century Danish-planter attire.

The jumbies would appear and then disappear.

I just accepted it. I didn't want to think critically about it. And I was high enough to allow things just to happen, not to force myself to believe I understood.

These sightings were similar to Jesus' appearance to his disciples after His resurrection. Go back and read some of those. They're at the end of the gospels. They make no sense whatsoever. Sometimes the disciples are with Him for hours without knowing who He is. Then they recognize Him and He disappears. Sometimes He's not in the locked room with them, and then suddenly He is. It's totally unbelievable weird-ness.

Any reasonable person would not buy it.

To make myself more comfortable, I spent a lifetime just ignoring the Gospels altogether. I'd fly right over the ridiculous reality and stay comfortably in my reasonable- my reasonable-

My whatever-the-fuck-it-is.

This is the same way I first interacted with the jumbies who began to appear to me in those months on St. John. I just ignored them.

Then once, when Prospero and I were smoking a joint in the bushes behind Skinny Legs' bar, one of the jumbies reached out and stroked my cheek in wonder.

I felt as if a stone-cold corpse had caressed my face.

And I asked Prospero, "What the hell, dude?"

"Jumbies," he said. "You've been seeing them for a few weeks now."

Somehow, I was o.k. with that.

He was right. I had been seeing them regularly. It's not that hard to accept something when you've been seeing it for a while.

A few months ago, before Joyce threw me out for good, I was sporadically dozing in front of the TV at our home back in the States. The documentary I had selected wasn't very interesting. I had mowed the lawn earlier that day, and Joyce was working on a remodeling project at the other end of the house.

Then an image appeared on the screen that was exactly something I had seen before. I sprang awake.

You've seen it described before in this book, in a poem I wrote as a very young man.

On the screen was a statue of the Virgin Mary in Seville, Spain. The statue is called the Virgin of the Macarena, or the Virgin of Hope. The Macarena was being carried out of a church by a faithful throng during a lavish festival. The people paraded the Virgin through Seville.

Illuminated by banks of candles, and moving with a quivering, human gait, the Virgin appeared to be quite alive. Her movement was transmitted by the people carrying her statue underneath. (The carriers were hidden by a drapery,)

Really, she appeared to be more than alive. She appeared to be supernatural, for the utter lack of a better word.

In the documentary, some spectators broke into tears at the sight.

The virgin was dressed in the most elaborate, golden robes.

Those robes are simply stunning in reality. They exceed my ability to describe them.

She doesn't have a crown so much as a universe of golden heaven surrounding her.

This is how she appeared to me when I was a young man. Joyce lay pregnant in the bed beside me. I couldn't see how things would turn out well. I thought all would surely not end well.

Yet the Virgin came to me and told me it would all be well.

That is the truth.

Now I have a bit more of a story to go through with that truth. It's a pretty damn messy story, as you have seen, and it's almost impossible for me to see how it could still turn out well in the end.

I want to share a confession with you.

When I took you into the bushes on Whistling Cay with Francis Bay and the jumbie, I didn't want to go in there.

I was terrified to go in there.

But there's this thing I've discovered about writing a novel. You sit down every day and you type away. A lot of it turns out to be no good. You have to throw it away. Some of it is o.k. You can rework it and rework it and rework it, and rework it a

lot more, and after a while you polish some good to the surface.

And then there are some days... There are damned few of
them. They just come of nowhere.

You sit down to write, and the words come pouring out like
magic.

I can't describe how that works.

It's like you finally just got out of the way, and the truth
came.

That's what I found on Whistling Cay.

Now: part of me wants to take all the bloody, dangling
threads of this story, weave them into a satisfying tapestry,
and-

What?

Could I throw my book off the cliff at Mary's Point and
drown it- as Prospero drowns his book at the end of *The Tempest?*

That's the way Shakespeare ends his play. Here's what
Shakespeare has Prospero say about that:

Our revels now are ended. These our actors,
As I foretold you, were all spirits and
Are melted into air, into thin air:
And, like the baseless fabric of this vision,
The cloud-capp'd towers, the gorgeous palaces,
The solemn temples, the great globe itself,
Ye all which it inherit, shall dissolve
And, like this insubstantial pageant faded,
Leave not a rack behind. We are such stuff
As dreams are made on, and our little life
Is rounded with a sleep. Sir, I am vex'd;

I too, am vex'd.

Miranda is coming to my boat tomorrow. The real Miranda. The real boat.

In the real Francis Bay, for God's sake.

Miranda and I (and you?) might be imagining an enticingly satisfying ending there. A consummation devoutly to be wished?

But that's not how this story ends.

The real fire in my loins is too compelling for that twist in the tale, as appealing at it might seem.

No. I've ultimately got to face the facts:

In truth- the light of my life makes her unwonted appearances in robes of inchoate, golden mystery.

And last night she told me this was precisely what she had wanted me to write.

The End

Also by Marshall Evans

FNNF-able

The Wheelman: *How the Slave Robert Smalls Stole a Warship and Became King*

Ten Tales of Improbable Escape: *Stolen from the Thief Giovanni Boccaccio*

Available wherever books are sold.

www.MarshallEvans.net

www.ingramcontent.com/pod-product-compliance
Lightning Source LLC
Chambersburg PA
CBHW030106260626
47156CB00008B/2550